'Emma...' His eyes blazed as he spoke my name.

His hand came up. My body went rigid. I held back the tears. I would not let him see the depth of my terror.

'Such soft skin,' he said.

He touched my cheek. The tips of his fingers trailed all the way around my face in the caress of a lover.

He smiled at me, a smile that was both cruel and lascivious.

It was then that I realized what he was going to do....

Hawkridge

by Jane Blackmore

ace books
A Division of Charter Communications Inc.
A GROSSET & DUNLAP COMPANY
360 Park Avenue South
New York, New York 10010

HAWKRIDGE

Copyright © 1976, by Jane Blackmore

All rights reserved. No part of this book may be reproduced in any form or by any means, except for the inclusion of brief quotations in a review, without permission in writing from the publisher.

All characters in this book are fictitious. Any resemblance to actual persons, living or dead, is purely coincidental.

An Ace Book, by arrangement
with the author

First Ace printing: September 1976

Printed in U.S.A.

Other Ace Books by Jane Blackmore:

AND THEN THERE WAS GEORGIA
ANGEL'S TEAR
BEWARE THE NIGHT
BRIDGE OF STRANGE MUSIC
BROOMSTICK IN THE HALL
THE CRESSELLY INHERITANCE
THE DARK BETWEEN THE STARS
THE DEEP POOL
THE MISSING HOUR
MY SISTER ERICA
NIGHT OF THE BONFIRE
NIGHT OF THE STRANGER
THE SQUARE OF MANY COLOURS
STEPHANIE
THREE LETTERS TO PAN
THE VELVET TRAP
A WOMAN ON HER OWN

CHAPTER ONE

THE SOUND CAME to me in my dreams, and yet I knew that I wasn't dreaming. I heard the beat of horse hooves both in my mind and in my ears. The clatter of metal shoes on macadam mingled with the rataplan of rain.

I shot upright. For a moment I didn't know where I was. There were walls, a floor and a ceiling, but the windows were without curtains or glass. The room was without carpet or furniture.

I stared at the open doorway. Rain lashed past. Beyond the streaming water I saw the grassland slope down into a valley and dissolve into the opaque distance.

The hooves were beating closer. I froze. The phantom hearse of my father's many-times-told legend was galloping up the hills towards me. The black hounds racing at the wheels, the black plumes leaping like flames from the horses' heads, the black six-in-hand horses soundlessly racing through the night to gather up the souls of the dead. My father's soul had been taken to his ancestors six long months ago.

Were the black horses coming for me?

Later, a long time later, I would recall this moment

of premonition. Now the note of alarm was gone. I was suddenly fully awake. Whoever it was that was coming up the hill was no phantom. I could hear the steady trot of the horse as clearly as I heard the drumming of the blood in my ears.

I'm not of a nervous disposition but as I took in the significance of my position in this isolated, derelict farmhouse, I felt panic. A flesh and blood man could be more dangerous to me than a phantom hearse. If only I had persevered with my judo! My gaze flew round the room. There was nothing, not even a piece of broken glass.

I sprang to my feet and stared at the doorless doorway. The goose pimples over my skin had been a delicious sensation when I sat on my father's lap in front of a bright fire and he told me his tales of mystery and mayhem on the moors. But, as I waited for whoever, or whatever, to appear I learned that the reality of fear was far from pleasant.

Murder! My father's stories had included several young females who had come to an untimely end at the hands of jealous or wild-living males. I had no wish to add my own death to the centuries of legends. No wish to be dropped down a mine or thrown into a bog. I couldn't move. I tried, but the beat of the horse's hooves stunned me. I was backed up against the wall of what had once been the kitchen of the farmhouse. I stared at the rain-lashed doorway. And I waited. . . .

Aunt Victoria had warned me about the dangers of the mists that come swiftly and silently over the heather and obliterate the hills and valleys.

Only this morning, at breakfast, she said it all again.

'Take care, Emma.'

'I do.' I sighed. 'Daddy told me many times about

when *he* got lost on Dunkery,' I repeated, parrot-like. 'If it happens, turn uphill beyond Dunkery Gate. You'll come to the road. Turn left and . . .'

'It's no laughing matter.'

'I'm sorry, Aunt Victoria.'

My Aunt Victoria didn't answer. She is so different from my father it's hard to believe they could have been born of the same parents. But then, of course, there are all the ancestors, with genes that provide endless permutations.

My father was a true Woollacott. His fine-boned face, strikingly blue eyes and pale yellow hair that recedes rapidly and early from high temples, all of these features are to be seen in the pictures of his father and grandfather and in the paintings of three generations before.

They can be seen in me. As a child I had the Woollacott white skin, long ashen hair and slim body. Only my eyes were a gift from my mother. The woman who had given me birth, and who I had never seen, for she died in the effort, looked back at me from green eyes, set deep and thickly lashed, every time I looked into a mirror. Now, my skin is not so luminously pale. My hair, still long, has deepened a couple of tones and features natural streaks of gold that would cost me a weekly fortune at the hairdresser to duplicate. I'm still inclined to be too thin around my arms and legs but the rest of me has filled out as a woman should. My eyes are still my mother's green.

My father was tall and quiet. My Aunt Victoria is small and dynamic. She wears old jeans and loose smocks that she embroiders herself in purple shaded wools in the long winter evenings. Her hands are strong, her fingers long and beautiful. She is a sculptress and she is in the middle of modelling a head of me. If I had her talent I would be modelling her hands.

'I'm truly sorry, Aunt Victoria. I won't be foolish.'

She smiled at me, freely and fully. 'I worry about you.'

'Please don't.' I stiffened. 'I'll survive.'

'Of course.'

She withdrew into herself and I was contrite. 'I'm not going to Dunkery,' I said.

'Where *are* you going?'

'I don't really know. I just want to get up on a hill. To see space.'

'You'll see space all right from the Beacon!'

'And people. I don't want people.'

'Emma . . .'

'Don't! Please don't say anything! Not yet!'

'You can't cut yourself off for ever.'

'No.'

'We all have our share of the cross to bear.'

'Yes.'

Her eyes and voice softened. 'I know how hard it is for you, Emma.'

I couldn't give her back any warmth. 'I must go.'

'I've asked the Vicar to tea.'

I sounded hard but I couldn't stop myself. I was solid ice inside. One day, a word or a touch would thaw the frozen me and I pitied the person on whose head my desolation would flood. But it wouldn't be my father's sister, Aunt Victoria Woollacott of the tidy life, escaped from the world into her sculptures, her cottage and her church.

Look into her eyes. My father's voice was the voice of conscience.

But I didn't look into her eyes. I couldn't look into anyone's eyes. I couldn't take the pain of human contact. This was the reason why I had left my job and my friends, shut up my father's house and cut away my life.

'Of course,' Aunt Victoria said, 'I understand. Just one thing. I want you to tell me in which direction you think you may walk. It's a precaution that is necessary to take. However careful you are, it *is* possible to twist an ankle. I must ask you to understand my position, Emma. I live in Exmoor. If you should have an accident I must be able to give directions to the men who will have to come looking for you.'

I arranged a smile on my lips. 'I don't mean to be like a bear with a sore head.'

She began to speak, then changed her mind. 'And I don't mean to be a dominating hostess! The artist is an egoist! It's been selfish of me to keep you in the studio when the beauty of our moors is waiting for you.' She stood up from the breakfast table with its litter of empty egg shells, crumbs of toast and cups of tea-dregs. 'And don't argue. I'm happy to have you here with me for as long as you can stay. After the head, which I'm doing for myself, I've a commission from Crispin Brett. It's a long-standing order. He wants a figurine in bronze. You've got just the body I've been waiting for.'

'You mean naked?'

'Of course!' Her eyelids narrowed. 'You're not ashamed of your body, are you?'

'No, Aunt Victoria. I'm not. I just—' I lifted my hands in a small gesture. 'I just never thought it was statue material.'

'Well, I think it is.'

'And who is this Crispin Brett?'

'A friend.'

In the five weeks I had been living with my Aunt Victoria at Westwater Cottage I had learned one thing about her. When she didn't want to talk, she wouldn't talk. It was a quality I both understood and respected.

So now, as I heard the note of finality in her voice, I said, walking out of the cottage, 'I'll leave the car at Brendon Two Gates.'

Spring comes later at Exmoor than it did in my father's house on Richmond Hill but in the past weeks the green spears had pushed up high out of the beds beside the path. Any day now a host of golden daffodils would trumpet their song and bees would go on an early honey hunt.

'There's rain in the wind,' my aunt said.

'I'll walk to the Hoar Oak Tree.' I got behind the wheel and slammed the door. 'I can't get into any trouble that way.'

I turned the key and got into gear and accelerated. It was just as I shot forwards, the tyres skidding on the road, that she called out to me. Most of what she said was lost in the noise of my violent departure but I heard, '... watch out ...' and a man's name. A name with such robust and romantic undertones that I sang it to myself in a tuneless composition of my own all the way to Brendon Two Gates. And then, as I got out of my car and walked across the cattle grid, he fell out of my mind. Everything fell out of my mind. The evil and hideous death by violence suffered by my father, my own anguish and the bitter helplessness, all the hostility and despair that had made me a prisoner in London fell out of my mind as I climbed the long slope of the first hill.

Sheep turned to watch me with straight black stares. If I went even one step too close they turned and bounced with twitching tails to a safe distance and turned to stare again. It had been like this in London. At our home on the top of Richmond Hill. At the shop in Jermyn Street where I had spent not even the whole of one year, three hundred and thirty-four days to be exact, as assistant and pupil of my father. People, like sheep, staring at me, the pity even more difficult to endure than the curiosity.

I broke into a run. Just for a moment I had been free. Now it was all inside me again.

I went, slipping and skidding in a reckless effort to outpace my thoughts, down the steepening slope. It was the last day of April, and the tourists had not yet come. If I fell I would have to lie until Aunt Victoria sent men to carry me back on a stretcher. I ran faster. Physical pain would be a relief. I wouldn't have to make decisions in a hospital bed.

I came to the deep chasm of the valley where Farley Water runs sweet and clear between the tall grasses, singing along its bed of stones.

I bent and put my fingers in the water. I lifted them and brushed my forehead with cool water. Out of the corner of my eye I caught a flash of yellow and was just in time to see a wren flitter away from me and into the grass on the other side of the stream.

I raised my head. Towering above me, green and challenging, was the next slope. I crossed the water on stepping stones, took a deep breath and charged straight up the two-in-one hill. Ten minutes later I flung myself flat on the summit drinking in great gulps of air and waiting for my heart to stop trying to leap out of my chest.

It was when I sat up that I saw the storm clouds sweeping up the sky from Brendon Common. I leaped to my feet. Even as I watched, the far hill was disappearing beneath the rain. The storm would devour my car long before I could reach it. I wasn't afraid, there was no chance of losing my way for all I had to do was to keep close to the stone wall back to the road. It was simply that my mac was still on the passenger seat and I had no liking for a soaking.

I turned and measured the distance down the hill to the derelict farmhouse. The sun still shone on it, turning the spring green on the trees that sheltered it to gold. If I ran I could possibly reach it before the storm caught me.

I hesitated. The choice was simple. Go back, through a wetting, to the security of my car, a quick drive back to Westwater Cottage and tea and Aunt Victoria. Or go on, down the hill, probably dry, to sit out the storm in an empty, isolated, half fallen down building.

I chose the latter.

And in that choice lay the beginning of love . . . and the seed of danger.

The clatter of the horse's canter kept me transfixed, as stupid and stupefied as a rabbit caught in the lights from a car.

There were memories in me that I didn't recognise. Dark nights, women clutching babies to their breasts, men reaching for guns, the sound of 'The Gentlemen' galloping by. Something old and mysterious flowing on the wind. Something primitive beating the blood in my veins in rhythm with the beat of a horse's hooves.

The sounds dropped to a walk. My heart stopped.

A cantering horse was headed towards its destination and would go on by the house. This slow beating, hollow sounding, clip—clop, clip—clop, was surely coming towards me.

And then there was no sound.

I listened. Beyond the rataplan of the rain there was silence.

I shrank further against the wall. It was cold and damp. I waited. Nothing. Only the rain and the silence. Maybe what I heard *was* the phantom hearse of my father's legend. Maybe I was going quietly out of my mind and, when the men found me in response to Aunt Victoria's directions, they would have to take me off in a strait-jacket.

Maybe, nonsense! Ghosts didn't like charging around in the daytime any more than they enjoyed a drenching! It was a flesh and blood man out there on a flesh and blood horse. I had attended eleven classes in the art of judo. I could protect myself.

He came into the doorless doorway. His body filled the space, blocked out the light and the world. I couldn't see the horse but I knew it was there.

For a long time we looked into each other's eyes, the man and I.

My breath came out on a sharp high note of rejection. 'Go away.'

Beyond the man the horse was startled and answered me with a sharp high whinny. There was a confusion of movements between the man and his horse and then, abruptly, the horse was quietened. The man led it, gently talking to it, gently holding the great head within his arm, into the room. Its hooves clattered on the stone floor and were silent as the man slipped the reins over a hook on the wall. The horse's ears went back and forwards and it rolled great eyes at me. The breath out of its wide dark nostrils was a stream of mist. Steam rose from drenched flanks, from gleaming chestnut-coloured flanks.

The man ignored me.

With his back to me he opened a small cupboard I hadn't noticed on the floor behind the shadow of the door. He took out a cloth and wiped his horse. The rain fell down the horse's legs in pools onto the floor. The man took a grey blanket from the cupboard and flung it over the back of his horse. He patted the shining neck and turned to me. 'It is *you* who are trespassing. *You* who must go away.'

He spoke quietly. There was authority in his voice. My instant reaction was to flare up at his assumption that I would go meekly at his command. My close-following reaction was to do just that, to walk away from him, to escape from even the minimal contact involved in the assertion of my independence. And beneath both of these a part of me was drawn to him by the magnetism of strength and power I felt within him.

A light flared in my mind. 'Alexander!' I cried, and the way I said it, it sounded like a laugh.

He stiffened. He was tall. Even in the gloom of the derelict room there was a fine air about him, a beautiful arrogance. The rain was wet on his face and on the black hair that grew thickly around the edges of his black hunting cap. He wore a thigh-length white Burberry, the broad shoulders were dark with rain. His riding boots were black and his breeches were stone-colored. He stood, motionless, controlled and remote, ignoring my carolling of the name.

I had felt a momentary relief at the thought that this was Alexander, the friend of my aunt, the man whose name she had called out as I made my tyre-screeching getaway, but now the relief was gone.

If it *was* Alexander, why did he just stand there, silent? I couldn't see his eyes beneath the shadow of the peak on his cap but I felt his gaze on me. I saw myself through his eyes: An aggressive young female in faded blue levis and polo-necked lime green thick-knit jersey. I wore no makeup. I had fixed my hair in two plaits hung down onto my breasts, tied them with scarlet bows. I had no handbag, it was in the Jenson, the keys were tucked in a pocket. Altogether, my credentials added up to a great big question mark.

Even so, his unhurried inspection brought the blood flaming into my cheeks. Before I could find words to express my fury at his scrutiny he answered me.

'Emma Woollacott.'

His voice sent a shiver down my spine that added to my ill-temper. I didn't want to feel it but I couldn't deny the evidence of my senses. My eyes and ears told me that here was a man with a deeply sensual attraction for women. My inner self, sending out radar signals like a bat flying through darkness, reacted to something that matched my own loneliness. I baulked at this. He was so clearly a man in control of himself and his destiny. And yet I couldn't rid myself of the message I was receiving.

This, too, added to my resentment. He had no right to stand there, charged with a physical magnetism that seemed to transform the derelict kitchen into a ballroom of glittering chandeliers, while, at the same time, he drew me with the emotional pull of a lost child.

I heard my own laugh. It wasn't a nice sound.

'What's funny?' he asked.

'You are Alexander?'

'Yes.'

'My Aunt Victoria warned me against you.'

'As she did me against you,' he rejoined.

I stared at him. 'She warned *you* against *me*?'

'Not *against* you.' He paused.

'What then?'

'*About* you.'

'You've lost me,' I said. 'I don't understand.'

'You look cold.'

I found that I was shivering. 'I am cold.' I shrugged. 'It looks all right in the movies but actually a stone floor is not the best bed to sleep on.'

He was coming towards me. His boots snapped on the stone floor. If he made any kind of slick or flirtatious response to my own inept use of the word 'bed' I would wither him with a glance. If he read me so far wrong as to think it was an invitation and not the result of nervousness I would hit him.

He took a silver flask from his hip pocket. 'Brandy,' he said and held it out to me.

I drew myself to my full height and my eyes were on a level with his shoulders. 'No thanks,' I said. There were still a couple of paces between us but he was between me and the doorway. He reached for me. I pressed myself back against the wall but I couldn't lift my head. I couldn't look into his eyes. 'I don't want your brandy! I don't want anything from you! Get out of my way and I'll stop trespassing!'

'Your teeth are chattering.'

'It happens all the time!'

'Ah!' he said. 'I get it!'

'Good!'

'You're a silly girl!'

'Thanks.'

'For your information I have no liking for stone floors either.'

'*You* think that *I* think . . .'

He broke in. 'Well! Don't you?'

'I don't know what to think.' I was suddenly tired. 'I just don't know.'

'Of course you don't, Emma—or may I call you Miss Woollacott?'

I smiled. With a single sentence he had dispelled my foolish fears and I could laugh at myself. Not much. Not for long. Just for a split second I was free and happy.

'You may call me whatever name you like! And I deserve it!'

'Some,' he agreed. 'Here.' He held up the flask again. 'It's not drugged.'

'Not even poisoned?'

An invisible shadow fell between us. 'Take a stiff drink,' he said.

He turned away. I watched him stride from me and the shroud of loneliness fell over me again. I flipped up the lid of the flask and put it to my lips. The metal was cool but the brandy ran like fire down my throat. I took a stiff drink.

He was pulling the blanket from the back of his horse. In a few moments he would mount the chestnut and go galloping out into the rain. I would see him for a moment and then he would disappear, and for a little while longer I would hear the sound of receding hooves and then nothing.

CHAPTER TWO

I TOOK ANOTHER, much stiffer drink. He was still here, with me.

He folded the blanket and laid it on the haunches behind the saddle. The horse was surprised. It set back its ears and sidled. The man quietened it with voice and touch. He lifted the reins from the hook on the wall and turned to me.

'Ready.' It was a statement, not a question.

I walked quickly across the room. 'Thanks for the drink.'

'You've had enough?'

I tipped the flask upside down. No more than a teaspoon of brandy splashed onto the stone.

'You've had enough.' he said, his voice without tone.

'I feel . . .' Suddenly the fumes filled my head. 'Whew! I feel fine! Abso-lute-ly terrific!'

'I'm not surprised.'

His voice was dry. 'Oh, hell!' I cried, 'I'm a selfish cow! I'm sorry. Truly, I am. I should've left you some. After all—it was *your* brandy.' I was getting muddled. 'I mean, you didn't put the flask in your hip pocket for me.'

'For emergencies,' he said.

I giggled. 'Is that what I am? An emer—' I couldn't finish. I controlled the slippery thing that was supposed to be my tongue and changed it to 'A pretty kettle of fish!'

'Not pretty,' he said.

His voice was quiet. I bridled. 'Oh, go to hell!'

'Beautiful,' he said.

I was silent. I couldn't look at him. I looked at the stone floor and at the dark patch of the last of his brandy and I wanted to cry. But I couldn't cry. The tears were dammed too solid, too deep, to be released by a couple of stiff brandies and a simple compliment.

'Come,' he said.

I didn't argue. There was no argument left in me. I followed Alexander and the chestnut mare out through the doorless doorway into the rain. He put the reins over the horse's head and swung up into the saddle.

'Give me your hand,' he said.

I stared up at him. He was far above me. 'If you think I can get up there . . .'

'Put your left foot in the stirrup.'

'I'm going back the way I came.' I took a step. The ground was treacherous. I straightened my back. Water streamed down my head and face. It was already sneaking between the collar of my jersey and my neck, but I had made my gesture and I couldn't go back on it. I steadied my feet on the unsteady ground and intoned, 'Up the hill and down the dale and I'll get to Brendon before you.'

He didn't answer.

'Well?' I challenged.

'It's your life,' he said.

He gathered the reins, the chestnut lifted instantly into a trot. It was happening as I had known it would. He was going. I would be alone again. I thought of the steep hill, an ice-slide with all this rain, and I ran after him. The grass was a quagmire. In an instant my shoes were pools of water in which my feet squished and sploshed as I weaved along the road.

'Alexander!'

He didn't stop.

I filled my lungs with air and yelled at his imperious back. 'Alexander! Wait for me!'

He turned the mare. As he came back to me I thought that I had never seen anything more welcome than this man and his chestnut horse awash with rain.

He reached me and reined the mare to a standstill. I looked up into his eyes, the briefest of contacts that lasted no longer than the touch of a butterfly's wings. It was Alexander who looked away. But, in that moment, we each of us gave and accepted something from the other, so that we both knew, no matter what lay ahead of us, there would always be a part of me that was his and a part of him that was mine.

'You look like a bedraggled chicken,' he said.

'You're not much to look at yourself!' I retorted.

He whipped off his hat in a sweeping gesture and planted it on my head. 'There,' he said and jerked its peak so that it was down over my eyes. 'The stirrup,' he said. His foot left the stirrup and I stood on tiptoe and lifted my own foot into the metal. 'Your hand,' he said.

Before I had time to feel any kind of response to this first human touch for seven endless isolated months I was up on the horse behind him.

'Ouch!' I wriggled and the mare shifted her feet.

'Now what?'
'I'm sitting on a cold rice pudding!'
'If you'd got up sooner my blanket wouldn't be wet.'
'Sorry!'
'Apology accepted!'
'You—you—'
'Put your arms round me.'

He held his elbows in the air. His body was close but so far, by leaning back on the great haunches behind and beneath me, I had evaded further contact.

'I'm okay,' I said.

He didn't argue. With elbows still at right angles he kneed the mare into a trot. I slithered. I bounced. I slipped sideways. Years ago, when I was five, my father took me on the cakewalk at a seaside fair. Only once. Never again. I was terrified. I screamed at the feel of the juddering world that threatened to throw me off onto the hard earth.

I was terrified now as the horse's rearend went up and down beneath me and I shuttled, ignominiously, up and down in response, but not in rhythm. I didn't scream. I capitulated. I flung myself against Alexander and gripped him around his chest with every last ounce of strength that was in me.

His arms came down on mine. At his touch the mare moved into a canter. He didn't speak. Warmth was generated between us and my body adjusted to the smooth rhythm of the horse.

I knew that this was me, Emma Woollacott, clamped firmly and vigorously to the man called Alexander, that we rode through the rain of an Exmoor cloudburst on the back of a chestnut mare. These were the cold facts of the situation. But facts are not everything and the blood of my father runs in my veins.

He was a bit of a romantic, my lovely father. He fed me with tales of mystery, he gave me the gift of great love stories, and he left me a legacy of magic.

So, now, I was the Bride of Lochinvar, Lorna Doone with John Ridd, Titania with Oberon. I was on the handlebar of a bicycle, laughing as I sang, 'Raindrops Keep Falling On My Head.'

'Emma!'

I came back to reality. The horse had stopped. The scent of flowers mingled with the rain. I lifted my head from his shoulder and snatched my arms from around him.

He said, 'I thought you'd gone to sleep.'

'No,' I snapped. 'Where are we?'

'At my cottage.'

I looked. It was a gingerbread cottage, only half awake beneath the pointed eaves. A low porch ran the length of the front and this was filled with tubs of wallflowers, tawny and gold, mingled with the yellow daffodils and the pale faces of white narcissi. A stream flowed between the road and the cottage and a stone bridge led to the path.

'How have you got flowers already?'

'It's very sheltered here.'

I looked again. A hill sloped gently around the back of the cottage, thickly wooded with beech trees, whose buds were a storm of spring green snowflakes just alighted on the branches. He was right. The air in this sheltered fold of the hills felt warm against my face.

His hand reached for me but I slid, clumsily, off the horse without his help. I had no idea of time. We could have been riding for a few minutes or a lifetime.

'What time is it?'
'Time for food.'
'I must get back.'
'I'll drive you after lunch.'
'Aunt Victoria will worry.'
'Not yet.'
'I should contact her.'
'You can phone. Door's not locked.'

With this parting shot Alexander walked the mare up and over the little stone bridge to disappear beyond the far end of the gingerbread coloured cottage. The rain had eased to a fine drizzle. My jersey was wet through. It clung to my back like some monstrous jelly fish. The front, where I had been pressed against Alexander was dry. My jeans were soaked. The lift of the brandy and the excitement of the ride were wearing off. I didn't know where I was. I was hungry. Altogether I was in danger of falling into a mood of deep depression.

I walked slowly, squelchingly, across the bridge and up the short path and opened the door of the cottage.

There was a fire in the grate, a flame-leaping log fire in a black wrought iron basket. I ran and knelt on the floor and held my hands and my face and my body to the heat.

Alexander came in from the back. 'Come upstairs,' he said. 'I'll fix you up with dry clothes.'

I sat back on my heels. 'How about the mare?'

'Gammon'll look after Samphire.'

'So you're not a bachelor on his own,' I said, teasing him a little because just the sight of him again was enough to set my heart singing and I was nervous that he might hear my song. Besides, if Alexander was going to continue having this effect on me every time he came into a room it was important to know if he was married.

He gave me a quick look. 'Gammon's my groom-handyman.'

He hadn't answered my question. 'Samphire.' I looked up at him. His eyes, I saw, were so dark a blue they were almost black.

'I like it.'

'That's good.' He raised his eyebrows. 'Are you ready to come upstairs now?'

'Sure!' I said. I got quickly to my feet. The staircase was steep and narrow against the wall behind him. 'What have you got here? One up and one down?'

'Two of each. This room and the kitchen down here. Two bedrooms and a shower room upstairs. Gammon and Nanny Dee have their own flat over the stable where I keep Samphire, and the garage where I keep my Jenson. Does that answer you?'

He was looking straight at me. It told me some of what I wanted to know about him, but not the main point. Without this keystone anything that Alexander and I might build between us was doomed to collapse.

I looked down. Behind my back I twisted my fingers around each other. I slammed a brake on my thoughts. I was fully aware of my own emotional vacuum. This was a dangerous time for me, for the wound left by my father's death was beginning to heal, and I was wide open, ready to fall in love. I must be careful. I must watch myself. I must *not* weave around like a strand of instinct-driven ivy. I must *not* attach myself to the first presentable male that comes within my line of vision.

'Ask me,' I said. 'I'll tell you anything you want to know about me.'

'I know all I need to know about you.'

'Ah! Aunt Victoria told you!'
'I'm wet and cold. I'm going to change.'

He turned to the stairs. The ceiling was low and he had to bend his head and shoulders for the first few steps. I didn't hesitate. I hurried after him.

He paused on the landing and looked down.

'This cottage must've been built for people my size. Look! My head just touches the ceiling.'

'You look right in the cottage, Emma.'

I do? Do I? Are you feeling the thump of your heart, as I feel mine? I could live here. I could wrap this little cottage around me. Around *us*.

Aloud, I said, 'I bet you say that to all the girls!'

It was a cheap thing to say. His eyes shut me out before he turned away. I ran up the stairs and followed him.

The room was almost filled by a king-size bed. Along the far wall there was a narrow built-in wardrobe and a chest-of-drawers in pine. There were masculine brushes and bottles. In the tiny dormer window there were no curtains, and the cover on the bed was an austere grey hessian that matched the walls and the carpet. No pictures. No photographs. No flowers. He slept in a vacuum.

It was in that moment that I saw Alexander as a person in his own right. Up until then I had been romanticising but, in that moment of insight, young Lochinvar's bride and all the rest of the legendary heroines flew straight out of the window. This was the bedroom of a living man, disturbing in its emptiness.

In the mirror fastened to the wall above the chest, I saw the bed. And myself.

'And I'm no Lorna Doone or Titania!' I muttered.

Alexander was bent over a drawer. 'What was that?'

'Bedraggled chicken!' I mocked my image.

He straightened. 'I apologise.'

'For being honest?'

'For being rude.'

I was silent. Alexander wasn't joking, he was genuine in his apology for the words he now thought might have been hurtful. In that moment I fell in love, totally, irrevocably and for ever.

I said, my voice sharp to hide my emotion, 'Are those for me?'

He looked down at the clothes over his arm as if he wasn't quite sure of why they were there. My heart leaped like a lamb on a bright March morning. Had I given myself away? And, if I had, what was his reaction?

I held out my hand. 'I'll take them.'

He looked at me. There was nothing in his face to tell me his thoughts as he came across the room.

I took the grass green shirt and the brown Daks.

'They'll do fine.'

'Your nose still looks blue around the edges.'

'Hardly a good colour scheme!'

'The water's hot. Take a shower. You'll find a towel in there.'

'How about you?'

'I'm okay. I'm used to the weather.'

I hesitated in the doorway. 'Thanks.' I said.

Alexander smiled for the first time. I smiled back at him. I wrinkled my blue-edged nose at him and turned and hurried into the shower room.

He was waiting by the fire when I came down the stairs. He stood with his hands held out to the warmth as the flames threw a leaping golden light onto his face. His shoulders slumped. He looked tired.

I had looked into the second bedroom. It was small and pink and empty. The drawers were empty, the wardrobe was empty. I sniffed but there wasn't a hint of perfume. Nothing at all, in either room, to give me a clue to the state of his personal life.

I ran down the stairs but he didn't hear me; whatever his thoughts were, they possessed him. I felt excluded; even, ridiculously, a bit jealous.

I planted my bare feet apart and kept my hands clasped on my hips. I had rolled up the trouser legs to my ankles and the shirt sleeves to my elbows but I was still swamped in his clothes. I had rubbed my hair and brushed it around my shoulders with the brush I found next to his shaving mirror. The top was still wet, sticking close to my head, but the ends were drying, curling above my breasts. His shirt was open at my neck.

'Penny for your thoughts.'

He jerked round. His eyes looked a me but he didn't see me. If there is such a thing as a daymare as opposed to a nightmare Alexander was clearly in one.

'Help!' I called. 'I need help!'

His eyes focussed. 'Hallo', he said.

'Have you got a piece of string?'

'String?'

'A belt! A tie! Braces! Anything to keep me from losing your trousers!'

He laughed. The tension went out of him and his face was young again. 'Of course! Won't be a moment!'

He moved quickly past me and I went to his place by the fire as he raced up the stairs. The door in the wall at the right hand side of the fireplace opened and a woman came in, carrying a tray. She stopped when she saw me. She was scarcely an inch taller than myself. Her ample figure strained against a dress of baby blue terrylene, and her cheeks were as round and as rosy as one of those out-moded country apples that never come into the suburban supermarkets. Looking into her eyes was like looking into a summer sky.

She inspected me with a shrewd glance but I felt no animosity coming from her. It was as if she said, so now you're here my girl I'll bide my time, but there are things I could say and, mark my words, if the time comes, I'll say them!

To which I replied, me too!

Alexander came running down the stairs. He threw a green tie to me and as I wrapped it round my trousers he took the tray from the woman.

'I'll lay the table, Nanny Dee.'

'Very good, Master Alex.'

'This is Emma,' he said.

She inclined her head in royal acknowledgement. Whatever else might go on at this cottage, Nanny Dee reigned over its inmates as she had once ruled the nursery. I must take care to mind my manners or Nanny Dee would give me a swift rebuke.

She went back through the swinging doors. Alexander put crockery and cutlery on a small table in the window. I looked at the daffodils and beyond at the rain. I listened to the rain on the roof, falling now and then down the chimney, hissing on the logs. We were shut in by the rain. It created an intimacy that would not be the same if the outside world were ablaze with sunshine.

Nanny Dee came back. She put the things on the table in the window. She chattered comfortably about the rain and the man Gammon who I now learned was her husband and who, she said, was turning into 'a regular old fuss-pot!' The way she said it was as if she gave him top marks for being a good boy. The chatter of her loving irritation was as warm as the fire in the hearth.

With a smile that drew us together she left us alone. Alexander motioned me to the chair opposite to his. We ate brown-shelled eggs and crisp brown toast, followed by tomatoes and Stilton cheese out of a stone jar and crunching cool celery. We moved to the chairs beside the fire and drank coffee so hot it burned the tongue, and brandy in great bowled glasses.

When Nanny Dee wasn't physically present I was aware of her in the kitchen. It was as if she appointed herself my chaperone. I corrected myself. That wasn't what I saw in the bright blue eyes. Her role was more of a watchdog. Was she watching me or Master Alex? And just why should she feel it necessary? What was it that she knew about him? For one thing was clear in the present situation: Nanny Dee knew nothing at all about me.

But I didn't think of this until later. At the time I thought only of the warmth of food and fire, and of Alexander, and our talk which was easy and full of laughter.

And then the telephone rang. The shock of the bell made my stomach tighten and my nerves jerk and the outside world came jangling into the room. For an hour I had forgotten my own loss, I had forgotten to think of my father, we had, both of us, kept out talk impersonal, and I had been happy.

Now it all came back to me.

Alexander reached out and lifted the phone on his fingers from an open shelf beside his chair. Had he been happy? Certainly he had seemed to be so. Now, the lines tightened in the muscles of his face. He half turned from me and his voice was cold. He went straight in. Clearly he knew who it would be, that words would be said.

'I got caught in the rain . . . Yes, Nanny Dee is here and she's boiled me a couple of eggs. I should've phoned but . . .'

The voice came to me out of the earpiece, distorted and distraught. I couldn't hear the words but I felt myself to be an intruder. I made a small move, raising myself away from the back of the chair. Alexander didn't look at me. He lifted his hand in a half-hesitant gesture and let it fall back on the arm of the chair again.

I couldn't go, nor could I sit here, listening, so I got up and walked to the door. I opened it and stood on the verandah. The rain slanted by, pitting the surface of the puddles, dissolving in the hurrying waters of the stream. I put my hands up to my ears but a sudden anger in his voice kept them away and I went on listening.

'No one! . . . I already said, Nanny . . . Who told you? No, don't bother to lie. I know my cousin . . . All right! I'll be back . . . About an hour.'

The phone gave a small click as he replaced the receiver. I waited a moment and then I turned. Alexander was on his feet.

'Sorry about that,' he said.

'What for?'

'The interruption.'

'That's why the telephone was invented.'

'I should've taken it off the hook.'

'Do you often cut yourself off?'

'Only . . .' He stopped, changed his mind and said, 'You do know, Emma, that I . . .'

My heart thumped. 'I know,' I said lightly, 'that it's

time I went back to Westwater. Aunt Victoria'll be having kittens.'

'You can phone her,' he said with a twist of his lips.

I looked him straight in the eyes. He held my look and I saw no embarassment nor confusion in him. Whoever it was, and of course it was a woman, I didn't want to know, not now, not here. I wanted to keep this hour safe, to have it as a place to which I could retreat.

'Yes,' I agreed, 'I could.'

'But you're not going to.'

'No.'

'I'll get the car and drive you to yours.'

'Thanks.'

He did't move. And I didn't move. We just stood there looking at eath other while my heart hammered against my ribs.

He said, 'Nanny Dee'll wash your . . .'

'Heavens! I forgot! I'll fetch them while you get the car.'

I ran from him, up the stairs and into the shower room where I collapsed onto the stool and waited for my heart to calm down. When it was quiet and steady and I could no longer feel it, I went back down the stairs, my wet clothes cold over my arm.

Nanny Dee was by the table. If she had intended to pretend a busy clearing of our dirty utensils she was too late. She was staring out of the window. I could hear the hum of the engine but I couldn't see the car or the man.

I spoke her name and she jerked round.

'I didn't mean to make you jump.'

She said, speaking fast, her voice low, 'It's not right to have favourites.' She glanced out of the window, assuring herself that he wouldn't come and turned back to me. 'I tried not to but Master Ulysses was a baby that cried. Was always crying. We got no peace. Only Master Alex could quiet him. There was always something close between the two boys. I couldn't help myself. Master Alex was such a bonny child. Always laughing. Not goody-goody! Oh, dear me, no! Master Alex was as full of mischief as any healthy boy. But never wicked.'

She came close to me. 'I could tell you things!'

'Do you think you should?'

Her eyes pierced mine. 'A changeling. That's what we got in Master Ulysses.'

'Oh come, Nanny Dee . . .

'You can laugh.'

'I'm not laughing. I just can't believe . . .

'Then you'd better believe. The moors are beautiful but there are dark places up there where murder and magic . . .'

I broke in. 'We have dark places in London!'

'You think I'm a silly old woman but I was as young as you when I first saw Master Ulysses in his cradle. A lovely fair-haired baby with rosy cheeks. Just what the fairies wait for to snatch.'

In spite of myself I felt a shiver race up and down my spine for this was one of my father's tales. When he first told me, I had looked in the mirror to assure myself that I was still blonde and healthy and wasn't turning into some withered old woman. Or worse, that I might see my features grow dull and brown as I saw that I was a carved piece of wood left by the fairies in place of the human baby I had once been. Maybe, I had thought, my dead mother had wanted me, and, not wanting to leave my father alone she had bribed the fairies to take me to her and leave a changeling in my place. It had taken several months before the busy days at school had finally routed my fears as I saw that my face remained the same.

Now, looking into the troubled eyes of Nanny Dee, it all came back to me. It was nonsense, of course! But her concern came from a troubled heart.

'Why are you telling me?' I asked.

'To put you on your guard.'

'Against this Ulysses?' I broke into laughter. 'For heaven's sake! He can't really be called Ulysses!'

'And that's another thing. At the christening. Right by the font. As he was handed to the Vicar his mother's voice rang out. "No!" she cried. "Not Crispin!" There was a strange look on her face. "Ulysses! My baby's to be called Ulysses!"

I could see the scene in the church. There was Crispin Brett, the man my Aunt Victoria had told me had commissioned her to make a figurine of a girl, his wife at his side with exaltation on her face, the godparents and the Vicar staring at her as she shouted. The baby in a long lace and voile dress, the heirloom that had gone off-white, with his golden hair and rosy cheeks and healthy squalling lungs. I couldn't see Alexander.

'Where did his brother stand?'

My thoughts returned to the room with a start. 'Alexander.'

'They're not brothers. Cousins. Mr. Crispin and Mr. Christian, fathers of the boys were brothers. Twins. Mr. Christian and Mrs. Christian died six months ago. In that plane crash. Remember?' I nodded. 'Where was I? Ah! Master Alexander wasn't at the christening. Well not as you mean. He was born that very night. It was that night that I began to see changes in the baby

Ulysses. His hair went darker, redder, from that very night. And his eyes began to lose their blue-heaven look. I'll swear he looked at me that night when we heard Master Alex give his first cry. Straight in the eyes, Master Ulysses looked at me. And he stopped his own squalling, just for a moment, and grinned.'

'Wind!' I said, but I didn't believe my own diagnosis.

Nanny Dee's face came back to normal. She gave me a conspiratorial smile. 'Most likely it was. He was a greedy baby and always overfilled his stomach if he got the chance. But there was something in him the night Master Alex was born.'

'Competition,' I said.

'Competition!' Nanny Dee sniffed. 'More like armed combat.'

'Little boys fight.'

'Of course! But not all the time! Even in the nursery Master Ulysses had to have his own way. He'd snatch Master Alex's toys.'

Perversely, I was beginning to enjoy the image of the truculent little boy with the red hair and dark eyes. Beside him 'Master Alex' was pallid and a trifle dull. 'I suppose Alexander just sat and cried for you.'

'Master Alex!' Her eyes flashed. 'Don't you believe it! Many's the time I've seen the bumps and bruises on Master Ulysses to prove that Master Alex was no coward.'

'Coward? Oh come, Nanny Dee! They were only two little boys working off steam.'

'You weren't there, Miss Woollacott.' Her lips shut tight.

'No,' I agreed. I lifted my shoulders in a brief shrug. For a moment she looked at me and I thought she wouldn't tell me any more about her 'boys', but she went on as if under a compulsion she couldn't stop.

'You must understand,' she said. 'Master Ulysses was born six weeks before Master Alexander. But Mr. Christian was born six minutes before Mr. Crispin.'

'So what Ulysses gained on the swings he had already lost on the roundabouts.'

'But Master Ulysses never accepts that he has lost.'

I smiled at Nanny Dee. It might well be that she was made jumpy by the shadows of her own vivid imagination. It was certain that she was deeply disturbed, filled with an apprehension that had thrust her into this intimacy with a stranger.

'Don't worry,' I said. 'You told me yourself that Alexander packs a powerful punch.'

'I love that boy, Miss Woollacott.' She didn't raise her voice but it was a shout of joyous acclamation. And then she said an unexpected thing, something that set a small song in my heart. 'You are the first. I've been waiting for you. Never forget, you are the only one he has brought to Kitnore.'

Before I could answer, Alexander's voice shot between us.

'Gossiping!' He smiled at her. 'Really, Nanny Dee!'

She swung round and faced him. She was a little woman, but in her passion she seemed to outsize the man.

'You can Nanny me as much as you like, Master Alex, but I know what I know!'

He came to her and put an arm around her shoulder. 'And gossip is part of the woman scene!'

'Men don't gossip!' I mocked him, rushing to the aid of Nanny Dee.

'Of course we do. But about markets not memories.'

'Things,' I scoffed, 'are not as important as people.'

He grinned at me. 'We've got a young vixen with us, Nanny Dee.'

'And you'd best watch your step Master Alex or Miss Woollacott'll go to ground and you won't see her again.'

We were suddenly quiet. The grin went off Alexander's face. Nanny Dee stood motionless within the circle of his arm. I felt her watching me but I didn't respond, for Alexander looked at me and there was power and passion in his eyes.

Abruptly, the flame between us burned out. It was a wet afternoon. I was tired and depressed. I had listened to an old woman's nursery gossip as if she spoke words of the highest wisdom. I had unfrozen a little at the fire of this man. Now I wanted nothing so much as to get away from both of them.

As if he read my thoughts Alexander said, 'Time to go.' He gave her a hug. 'I won't be back,' he said. 'I have to go on to Hawkridge. I've told Gammon to exercise Samphire.'

The pugnacity went out of her. 'You'll be lunching tomorrow?'

'I'll come,' Alexander said with another hug before he let her go, 'as soon as I can. I've got things to do tomorrow.'

'You take care, Master Alex.'

He laughed. 'None of your tea leaf reading mornings!'

Nanny Dee turned to me. 'You too, Miss Woollacott. He can laugh at me. But murder has happened. And not a million miles from here neither.'

'Away with you, oh prophetess of doom!' He turned to me, laughing. 'Would you care to step outside into my

Jenson? Unless, of course, the old witch has turned it into a broomstick.'

'I'll broomstick you, Master Alex!' Nanny Dee retorted. 'And it won't be the first time I've given you six of the best on the bare behind!'

It was a cheerful exchange, an affectionate bandying of words, but I was still chilled. I said, 'Thanks for a superb meal, Nanny Dee,' hurried from the cottage that had been a brief haven, and got into his car.

Alexander ran round the back, got in at my side, and the bonnet of the car raced up over the hunchback bridge. My stomach hit the back of my throat as the car fell down the other side of the bridge.

I didn't look back. I didn't need to. I knew that Nanny Dee had come out of the cottage and was standing in the rain watching us.

I knew, too, that although I ached to speak the question, I would not ask Alexander what he was doing on the following day.

He told me as I stood on the road outside Westwater. He told me and slammed the car into a roaring start before I could answer him.

CHAPTER THREE

'Did Alexander tell you?'

It was after our evening meal. We sat in old and deep and comfortable arm chairs on either side of a coal fire. There were daffodils in vases and brandy in bowl stemmed glasses.

I was learning, it seemed, all the time. My Aunt Victoria had been in her studio at the end of the garden when I returned. It had once been a dovecot, large and round, constructed in weather-beaten stone and full of the throat-catching crooning of white doves. Now, the north side had been squared and replaced with a sliding patio glass door, very modern and wholly incongruous.

I was learning that nothing mattered to Aunt Victoria except her work. The present sculpture was the centre, the absolute essence, of her life. She saw no friends, read no newspapers. I felt that I, too, spun on a distant periphery. I was in awe at her total dedication. In comparison my own artistic impulse was a puny thing.

When Alexander left me after telling me his plan for tomorrow I looked for my aunt. I saw her, at the end of the garden, a squat dun-coloured overalled figure beyond the glass, and I knew that I needn't have worried. My Aunt Victoria was not like my father. Having asked me to visit she had done her duty, fulfilled an obligation to the child of her dead brother, but I was not to enter her life, there would be no anxious questions nor any frightened rebukes. This freedom was what I had wanted, what I had fought my father about on many occasions when I had come home late. I could hear myself, shrill and kicking against the traces.

'For goodness sake, Daddy! Stop crowding me! I'm grown-up.' This when I was sixteen. At seventeen, 'I only went on to a party! No, it wasn't a sex-and-or-drug orgy! Just a beer and sausage do!' I always talked at him in exclamation marks in those days. At eighteen, 'I'll be in college in six months, Daddy! You've taught me all I know! Now, relax! If you can't have faith in my judgement at least have hope! Even a little charity!' I was pleased with myself for that one!

And then he died. Was killed, instantly, on a bright September afternoon by some tearaway who passed a car at speed on a corner. A split second earlier or later and my father would still be alive. And I would have had time to tell him that at nineteen, after twelve months at Cambridge, studying Art and Social Sciences, I understood his fears and was even made happy and secure by the reins of love he still kept on my headstrong impulses.

He died. The unspoken words were an ice pack of guilt and misery within me. Death was so final. It could be right, even good and beautiful, if it came quietly at the end of a life lived to its natural climax. Death by violence was evil. Ugly. It left the living filled with despair. The need to atone for the things left undone, for the unmeant rejection, for the thoughtless hurt, was an ever present pain from which there was no escape, no reprieve. For I could never say, 'Daddy, I'm sorry.'

That afternoon, running up the stairs and slamming the door of my room my loneliness was highlighted by my Aunt Victoria's disassociation. In grief I cried out to my father. If I could only hear his voice! I could see his face but his voice was silent. I could repeat his words, 'You're late. Where have you been!' but my ears couldn't hear the tone of his voice. I heard only the rain.

I hadn't known, until he was gone, how safe I had been. Now I had no traces to kick against, no one to care if I went out or came in. My Aunt Victoria lived her own life alone with the Pygmalion creatures that came out of stone and marble beneath the impact of hammer and chisel in her strong hands. She was kind but she would always be impersonal.

I had come here, to my father's sister, looking for contact. Now I knew that my way back to the world was not through Aunt Victoria.

Alexander? I couldn't think of him.

I could think of nothing but my loss.

I lay on my bed, still in his shirt and trousers, and fell asleep . . .

'Emma!'

I started. The bright little room came back into focus. 'Yes, Aunt?'

She gave me a small smile. 'Just like your father.'

'Am I?'

'Of course,' she said, as if even that small remark was too great an intimacy. 'I didn't see anything of him after he went to London.'

'Nor of me.'

'It wasn't easy.'

'I'm not criticising.'

'Someone had to look after our Mother.'

I stared at her. 'It was you who wouldn't let Daddy come.'

'I said it wasn't easy,' she repeated.

'You told him,' I persisted, 'when he wrote and asked if he could come and see her that she wasn't well enough. That a visit from him would kill her.'

'It's a long story, Emma. He was the apple of her eye. The day he left Exmoor she began to let go of life. I believed that the excitement would be too much for her.

'Grandmother must've known that he would go.'

'I'm not blaming him. I was the practical one. Your father was the dreamer. Thought he was going to change the world.'

'He made my world.'

'I'm sure he was an excellent father.'

'He was a good teacher, too! He taught a lot of kids to see beauty.'

'I'm not running him down,' she said. 'No, let me finish. We had different talents. We lived different lives. We were both poor letter writers. A card at Christmas. Sometimes, if we remembered, at birthdays. But he was my brother. Blood *is* thicker than water.'

A piece of coal shifted on the fire and a shower of sparks fell through the metal basket onto the bed of embers. There had been no blood on my father when, at last, I was allowed to see him.

I couldn't speak. The clamp had settled around my throat. I had hoped, prayed, that it would stop when I left the flat on Richmond Hill. I had had a few weeks of respite since I came to Exmoor. Now, at this first open talk of my father, it was back again.

Aunt Victoria said, 'We've got off the track. I find I'm inclined to do that when I'm working towards the completed job.' She laughed. 'Unless, of course, I am what the village say I am! That crazy sculptress!'

My throat was easier. I swallowed nervously, and found my voice. 'I—I can't talk about—him.'

'Don't force yourself. It'll come.'

'When?'

'One day. In the meantime let's talk about tomorrow when Alexander Brett is taking you to join in our own version of the spring fertility rite.'

'Is that what it is?'

Her eyes were shrewd, her voice dry. 'If it was Ulysses I'd know he had only one denouement in mind.' She shook her head. 'With Alexander—you never know what Alexander's thinking.'

'No.'

She looked across at me with penetrating concentration. She had looked like this when she was working on the head of me. I didn't mind it then. Now, I shrank into myself, shifted a little beneath the piercing gaze.

'Did Alexander tell you?'

'Tell me what?'

'So. He hasn't told you.'

I stared back at her. 'What's all the mystery?' I challenged.

Her eyelids narrowed. 'Emma,' she began and stopped short. 'Oh, hell,' she exploded. 'It's none of my business.'

'What isn't?'

'I will not get involved in the Brett family traumas!' She went on quickly, as if she couldn't stop. 'I made my choice when I was younger than you are now. There was

Mother. There was my work. Of course there were nights when I wept into my pillow. Times when I knew that life was passing me by. Days when I cried out to God. But because of my work I accepted my loneliness. And there were the letters. It was all made worthwhile when someone wrote of their happiness at living with one of my sculptures.'

She stopped and picked up the glass of brandy and drained it. She set it down again on the table and gazed into the fire.

'And you, Aunt Victoria?'

'Me?' she murmured, not looking at me.

'Was it the right decision?'

'I am content.'

'Happy?'

She looked up, laughing. 'If you mean do I greet each new dawn with a shout of delight—Well? Have you heard me?'

'No.' She was laughing at herself and I laughed with her. 'We're neither of us morning people!'

'But I feel joy,' she said. 'Not all the time. That way I would be mad! When I'm least conscious of myself. A flower. A bird singing. A storm blowing over the moors. A single absolutely right movement of the chisel in my hand. Any of these things. So many things. And I feel joy.'

She gave me no time to answer, none to feel if I *could* feel. She was on her feet. The crimson smock-topped gown hung to just above flat moccasins embroidered in brilliant greens and reds on a silver background. Her features were homely, her body thick, her movements ungainly, but there was on aura of shining calm about her that made her beautiful.

For the second time I was filled with envy of my Aunt Victoria. She had come through her own fires and was a whole woman. And then, as she smiled down on me, I knew that the answer for Aunt Victoria would never satisfy me. A life that was right for her could be drudgery and boredom for me. I wanted a husband and I wanted children. I wanted physical union and emotional communion. I wanted fights and lovemaking and I didn't want to spend my days at some advertising firm making designs to sell soap or soup or whatever.

It was a very ordinary thing to discover about myself. That I was a girl who was ripe for marriage. I didn't feel ordinary. I felt unique.

And then Aunt Victoria said, 'Alexander Brett is a very attractive man.'

I was on edge. 'Is that what you warned me against?'

'Warned you against? When?'

'When you called after me this morning.'

'Great heavens no! I only wanted to tell you that he rides that way, so you would know who he was.'

I didn't asnwer. I didn't ask the obvious question. If Aunt Victoria had said things to him about me I didn't want to hear them from her.

She was standing, going to the door. She looked at me and said, quiet and gentle, 'Don't fall in love with Alexander Brett.' She went straight on. 'Good night, my dear. I'll say a prayer that sleep comes easily to you.'

The door shut behind her. I sat and stared into the fire. Her warning, for this time the warning was clear, was too late. I could tell myself that I was a fool but I couldn't tell myself with any assurance that I wasn't already enough in love with Alexander Brett to sit and relive the words and moments of our time together.

Sleep didn't come until it was dawn and the birds began to sing. I was in a deep and dreamless non-existence when Aunt Victoria's brisk knock jerked me back to life.

She flung back the door, letting in a flood of energy. 'Wakey-wakey!'

I peered at her over the bedclothes around my chin, exhausted by the brightness she exuded.

'What's the time?'

'Nine-fifteen.' She was brisk but courteous. 'I overslept. Mustn't do it again. Late to work this morning. Not good enough.'

I sprang out of bed. 'I'm sorry, Aunt Victoria.'

'What for?'

'Keeping you up last night. It won't happen again.'

She softened. 'Silly girl! Not your fault. Mine! Well, I'm off now.' She shut the door behind her, then opened it and poked her head into the narrow crack. 'I presume he's taking you to lunch?'

'Alexander?'

'Who else?'

'I don't know. He didn't say. But don't worry. If he's got to get back for whatever I'll fix myself something to eat.'

My Aunt Victoria said, 'Fine! Fine!' and shut the door again.

I hurried to the bathroom. Half-past nine, Alexander had told me. The shower was icy. As I gasped and spluttered and turned my face up to the cold needles of water I came to a cold and sensible decision. I would go with Alexander Brett, I would join in the fun of the May Day Eve Hobby Horse. I would keep the contact light and I would enjoy myself. I would not ask him what it was my Aunt Victoria thought he should have told me about himself.

I dried myself and dressed in black levis and a new black sleeveless top that made the most of my thirty-four inch measurement. I was in such a hurry to be ready (my father had been strict on keeping to appointments) that I didn't have time to notice the double act that I and my subconscious were playing. I could decide to 'play it cool' but my inner self, the emotional self that had been aware of his awareness, had selected the most interesting and flattering top in my wardrobe.

I was in the kitchen pouring orange juice when the phone rang. I ran across the hall and into the sitting room and grabbed the receiver to my ear.

'Hallo!'

'Emma?'

It was his voice. My cold and sensible decision flew out of the window. 'Alexander! Isn't it a heavenly day? That storm really washed the sky biological blue!' He tried to speak but I wouldn't let him, there were so many things to be said. 'And talking of washing, I've done your shirt but I haven't ironed it yet. If you've rung to say you'll be late picking me up I'll get out the iron and have the shirt with a top laundry finish by the time you get here.'

I stopped at last. The line was blank. I tried to visualise him but I had never been in his house and I could imagine no background other than the cottage and I knew he wasn't at Kitnore.

'You still there, Alexander?'

'Yes?'

'I thought you'd given up!'

'I don't give up so easily.'

'I go on! I know I do! Specially when I'm . . .' I bit my lower lip. What could I say? Excited? Nervous? Enchanted by your voice? Suddenly afraid of why you've called? I finished, 'When I'm drinking orange juice.'

'Me too.'

I went silent. He spoke in a flat formal tone. What did he mean, 'me too'? Was he laughing at me? Or was there someone in whatever room he was in? Listening? Watching him? And if so, who?

He said, 'Emma!'

There was no flat formality in the way he said my name.

'I'm here,' I told him and went on quickly, forestalling him, for it was easier to say than to hear. 'You're not meeting me this morning.'

'I can't.'

I choked on my disappointment. 'No such word!'

'What's that?'

'Can't. There's no such word. My father told me.'

'Your father was wrong. There are times—circumstances—which add up to can't. I'm sorry.'

I had to ask. 'Do you mean it?'

'I said it.'

'It could be just a figure of speech.'

He evaded me. 'I don't want you to miss it so I . . .'

I broke in. 'Don't worry about me!' This was the second time in fifteen minutes that I had assured someone that they need not concern themselves with my welfare. It was getting to be a habit that I could easily dispense with. 'I'm fine!' I said. 'I'll go on my own!'

'If you'll let me finish,' he said, heavily patient, 'I'll tell you that I've fixed with Uncle Crispin to take you.'

'Uncle Crispin,' I repeated.

'He'll pick you up at ten.'

'And what,' I asked, matching his heavy patience with an equal weight of sarcasm, 'have I done to be sent to a spring festival with an elderly uncle? Why not cousin Ulysses?'

'Because,' he said, icily, 'I haven't asked Ulysses. But if that's what you want. *Ulysses!*'

His shout came out of the receiver and set my ear ringing. I snatched the phone from my head and put my hand to my ear but I couldn't shut out his voice 'Ulysses! you're wanted on the phone!' My strategy had worked. I had shaken Alexander from his social shell. I could hear the hurt in his angry shout. I called out to him but he didn't hear me.

I slammed down my own receiver. I went back to the kitchen and gulped down my orange juice. I didn't know now if Uncle Crispin would come for me. I decided that it was time to stop behaving like a spoiled child and behave like the civilised adult I liked to believe that I was.

I went and sat in the sun on a wooden bench beside the porch. I didn't have long to wait.

A black Rover came to the gate and out of it stepped Crispin Brett. I looked at him with interest for this was the man who had commissioned my Aunt Victoria for a nude statuette.

I knew at once that I could not sit for it. I'm no prude, nor am I ashamed of my body. In the pursuit of art the human body is an interesting challenge, as is an apple or a glass of water.

It wasn't shame or modesty that made me certain. There are people with whom one feels immediate contact, as if one had known them before. If anything convinces me that I have lived a previous life it is this inexplicable moment of understanding.

I had felt it with Alexander, but he was a young man and there were so many reasons for an instant reaction. Crispin Brett was not of my own generation, I felt no physical reaction, he wasn't at all like my father so it wasn't a substitute-figure. There was no reason why I should feel affection for him but I did.

I knew that he felt the same for me as he waited for me to go to him. His black homburg hat in one hand, the other hand resting on the top of the low gate, he smiled at me and said, 'Hallo, Emma,' as if it was only an hour since he had been with me.

I got up. 'Hallo, Crispin.'

I came to him and he smiled.

'Alexander told me you'd be ready.'

I ignored this. I would not discuss Alexander. 'You're not exactly tardy yourself!'

He pushed the gate and held it open for me. I waited for a split second while my mind took a picture of him.

The sun sparked lights out of his close-cropped iron grey hair. He had a neat iron grey beard and between this and the neat iron grey moustache his mouth was young. His back was straight, his shoulders square but there was a quality of innocence in his eyes that gave the lie to his outward appearance. And if I felt that there was weakness in his chivalrous spirit, in his lack of understanding that the world is full of wheelers and dealers it only made my own affection stronger.

He ushered me into the car and in a moment, it seemed, we were driving over Stoke Pero Common. He didn't talk, but as I looked out across the wooded valley to the distant hills I felt a little of his calm seeping into my troubled spirit. The road took a sudden turn and we were running downhill through a spring-green wood, full of twists and turns and shadows, past Luccombe beside a stream that raced, clear and bright, carrying yesterday's rain to the sea in Porlock Bay.

And then, as he turned the car onto the main road my mood changed. I wished I had come on my own. Alone I told myself, mocking my sudden longing for Alexander, I would have found a young companion with whom to celebrate the fertility rites.

We drove into Minehead. I hadn't seen a town for the five weeks I had lived at Westwater and now I found that the pavements and rows of houses were depressing. I shrank into myself. There were so many people. I didn't want to be hustled and shoved about in a crowd of bodies.

I shrugged. I had come to see the Hobby Horse. It would soon be over and I could go back to the moors.

Crispin Brett parked the Rover and ushered me through the streets. Miraculously, a way opened for us and at last we reached his selected vantage point. There were people lining the pavements but somehow, without fuss, he manoeuvred me into the front line. I stood there with the children and looked across the empty road to where more children with bright eyes and wind-rosy cheeks were wriggling and laughing in front of the crowd.

Beyond them was the sea, with a multitude of small waves, foam-crested, racing in from the horizon. The sun sparkled and almost took the chill out of the wind. The scent of the sea was sharp and the chatter of the children rose to shrill excitement.

'Can you see, Mr. Brett?' I asked, glancing over my shoulder.

'I've seen the Hobby Horse before,' he said. 'Don't you worry your pretty little head about me. Look! They're coming!'

As I turned to look there was a squeal from a small boy at my side. He hopped into the road. An elbow jarred my ribs. 'Jason!' a woman shrieked. 'Get back on the pavement! This instant! Get back!'

Subdued, crestfallen, sullen, the little boy came back to my side. I smiled down at him. There was the sound of music coming along the road.

'Listen!' I said, and, as the memory of my father's tales came flooding back, went on, 'Can you hear the magic music?'

The little boy gave me a look of contempt. 'It's Alf and Harry Stenner!' he said.

'It is?'

His contempt changed to wide-eyed rhapsody. 'I play the drum. Alf Stenner's teaching me. I'm to take his place. Soon's I'm old enough.'

'Old enough to know better!' the woman said behind me. 'That Alf Stenner! He's a great joker!'

'He's not! I am too! He said so!'

The woman spoke to a companion. 'Can't teach that boy no sense! It's his father! Always telling him fairy stories! His mother's no help, living in her own world. I try but what can I do?'

The little boy looked up at me. Uncertainty was in his brown eyes. 'Alf said so,' he said, half defiant, half afraid.

'I'm sure he did,' I assured him. I wouldn't look round. I didn't want to see the face of the practical woman who, against the boy's father, rode roughshod on a child's dream.

The little boy's head jerked round as the drumbeat rolled up the street.

'Alf!' Jason leaped up and down like a yo-yo. He couldn't have been more than four years old but his voice shrilled above the boom of the drum. 'Alf Stenner! Here I am! I'm here!'

The man with the drum spotted him. His face lit up and he came across the road in a weaving dance. He came right up close. He stood in front of the little boy and his drumsticks beat out a compulsive throbbing pulsing rhythm that set a wildness racing in my blood. In another moment I would have leaped in the air at the side of the boy.

Alf Stenner grinned at me. He tapped Jason on the head, beating out a silent roll with delicately wrist-poised sticks. Without the pulsating drumbeat I heard the accordion and the gathering shouts of the children.

And there it was, almost up to where I stood. The May Day's Eve Hobby Horse. The gayest, most magnificent hobby horse I had ever seen. Its great head nodding, with huge eyes and flaring nostrils, it came along the road, leaping and prancing, the whole of its painted nine feet length of canvas quiveringly alive, and coloured ribbons flying like flames in the sunlight.

A small hot hand grabbed mine. I glanced down. Jason's face was aglow but he didn't look at me, nor did he bounce up and down any more. He was absorbed, entranced, innocent. I looked away from his face for I was deeply affected and this was neither the time nor the place for the frozen tears to melt.

The children were clapping. Jason snatched back

his hand and joined in. The Hobby Horse was prancing away along the road. The beat of the drum and the singing of the accordion were fading. The crowd was shifting. A few children went leaping and dancing after the little procession.

I was on the point of turning to Jason when an arm came round my waist. In the same instant a hand came over my eyes. It blotted out the sea and the road and I was in darkness.

CHAPTER FOUR

I DIDN'T SCREAM except in my mind.

'Crispin?'

It was a question. The courteous and formal Crispin Brett would never be so impulsive as to play this child's game. Besides, the body to which I was firmly clasped was hard and young.

My heart skipped a beat, 'Alexander!' I whispered.

Even as I voiced my hope I knew that it wouldn't be Alexander. It wasn't his style, either, to come up behind a girl and seize her round the waist. Alexander was quiet and strong and straightforward. When Alexander made a move it would be face to face.

I stood very still. Emotions sped over me as fast as the foam-white wavelets raced across the sea. Surprise, hope, fear, and then anger.

'Let me go!'

'Not till you guess my name!'

My father's oft-repeated fairy story gave me the answer. 'Rumpelstiltskin!' I said. 'Now! Let go of me!'

The arm left my waist and the hand went from my eyes. I spun round, had to look up to see his face. The sun was directly behind him and for a moment, dazzled by the bright light in my eyes, he was a giant with a thick mop of ginger hair and a huge smile around spectacularly white teeth. And I knew that it was Ulysses Brett.

'No,' he said. 'Try again.'

I looked away from him.

The woman was already twenty yards or so along the road. She was going fast, away from the Hobby Horse, away from the two of us. She had Jason by the hand. He seemed to hang from the end of her arm, his little legs took huge leaps. He turned his head and she gave him a sharp pull so that he half fell before he found his feet again.

My nerves spat. Why should I feel so sure that Jason was being hustled out of our presence?

And where was Crispin Brett? The crowd was dissolving. I could see the grass of Butlin's playground but there was no middle-aged gentleman with iron grey beard and black homburg hat. Now you see him, now you don't! I thought. I was being manipulated. I could feel it in the marrow of my bones and I didn't like the sensation.

There were two courses of action open to me. I could continue to pretend ignorance, or I could throw down my challenge. I looked back at the ginger-haired giant who hadn't moved a muscle while I was looking and thinking, except that he no longer smiled.

'You know,' he said slowly, 'who I am.'

'Ulysses Brett.' I smiled up at him for his voice had the same deep note of Alexander's voice and for a moment I was thrown off balance. To cover up I said, 'What's happened to Crispin?'

'He was called away.'

'Called away?' I repeated his outrageous lie.

'Yes.'

'By who?'

'Me.'

I gave him a straight look. 'I don't know what game you're playing but, whatever it is, I'm not interested.'

He said, 'Your heart beat fast just now.'

I blushed, furiously. 'Do you really think—?' I broke off and sharpened my voice. 'If it did . . .'

'Oh, it did! I felt it beneath my hand.'

'If it did,' I repeated, ice-cold, 'it's because you made me jump.'

'I frightened you!'

Something in the back of his eyes reached out for me and I remembered the words of Nanny Dee. I didn't believe that this man could be her changeling but I shrank into myself, hiding my thoughts from the calculated probing of his mind. I didn't believe that fairies had come flying over the moors to exchange their own for the human baby but I felt a vacuum, something cold in him, that set him apart from the rest of us. I felt, too, that he was aware of this in himself, but I couldn't tell if he was dismayed or proud.

I only knew that it could, if circumstances went against him, make him an implacable enemy. And that I must never let him know that I was afraid.

So I said, 'You made me jump, that's all.'

He relaxed. He smiled. 'That's all I meant to do.'

'Where's Crispin?'

'Do you care?'

'As a matter of fact I do!'

'I see that the old charmer has been at it again!'

There was a bite in his words, 'Your father,' I said coldly, 'was, as you say, a charming companion.'

'Which I am not?'

'So far—no.'

'I thought you sounded like a girl who would enjoy a joke.'

I looked away from him, out over the racing sea. I didn't want to talk about Alexander. I certainly had no intention of letting Ulysses know that his words had been understood.

'I do,' I said, 'but not stupid pranks. I left the apple pie bed stage when I was ten.'

'I apologise, Emma.'

'Forget it.'

'No, I mean it. Please accept my apology.'

'Accepted.' His persistence was making me uneasy. He seemed to be trying to provoke a reaction from me and I didn't want to react. 'Where is Crispin?' I asked.

'Up on the moors by now.'

My eyes flew to his. 'On the moors.'

'Halfway back to Hawkridge Manor.'

'You arranged this between you?'

'Not exactly.'

'What does that mean?'

'My father's as stubborn as he is charming. Alex asked him to escort you. He'd never yield his place to me.'

'But he did.'

'Yes.'

'What did you say to him to make him less stubborn?'

'I told him that Deidre was in another of her hysterics.'

'Deidre?'

He grinned, as happy as a schoolboy who scores the winning goal. 'Dad won't know till he gets back that it's a white lie!'

'Another joke.'

The grin went. 'I had to get to see you, Emma.'

I spun on my heel and began to walk along the road towards the town. 'Now you've seen me,' I said, 'Goodbye.'

'Hey!' He was beside me in a couple of strides. 'Wait for me.'

'Where's the nearest garage?'

'What do you want a garage for?'

'To hire a car to get me back to my Aunt Victoria.'

I spoke with a slow defined enunciation of each word as if I spoke to a subnormal child. My barb went home.

'I'll drive you.'

'No. Thanks all the same, but no thanks.'

'But I fixed . . .'

'Don't think you can fix me, Ulysses!' I saw what I was looking for across the street. ''Bye again.'

I stepped off the pavement. There was a screech of tyres, a blast on a horn, and Ulysses' hand snatched me back. It was all over in a moment. The driver of the car shouted abuses and Ulysses silenced him with, 'Go to hell!'. The car went on and he turned to me.

'You all right, Emma?'

'Sure. I'm fine.' I was a little breathless. 'Thanks.' I drew my arm from his hand. 'I'll look this time.'

'I seem to be doing it all wrong. Saying all the wrong things.'

He looked crestfallen. 'We all have our problems.'

'Give me one last chance.'

I hesitated and was lost. 'My Aunt Victoria will be worrying.'

He laughed. 'Your Aunt Victoria won't give a thought to you.'

I grimaced. 'No.' I agreed. 'I don't suppose she will.'

'Then you'll let me take you to lunch.'

'I don't eat lunch.'

'You're not on a diet.' he said, looking me over.

'Of course not! I'm just not hungry.'

'How about your thirst?'

'It's active,' I admitted. 'I could do with a long cool lager.'

'I know just the place,' he said. 'My car's in the park up the road. Shall we go?'

I nodded.

I walked at his side but the day was empty. The music had finally died away in the distance, the magnificent heart-lifting Hobby Horse had pranced away out of sight, the little boy had been dragged up the road as if there was suddenly poison in my presence.

It was too much effort to argue any more. Alexander was a blurred memory. My curiosity about Deidre and her invented hysterics was lost in my general inertia.

I couldn't even remember the feeling that had provoked my urge to get away. It had been there, I knew, but like a finished pain, I couldn't recall the sensation. It no longer seemed important.

Ulysses Brett was as good a way to pass a blank hour as any other.

Now, I know that I should have trusted my instinct. I should have been warned by his urgency, by the deceit of his scheme to get me on my own, but it was flattering to the ego. I had been hurt by Alexander's unexplained jettisoning of our day together and it was healing to be sought out by another young man. I needed the lift he offered me, both the mental fillip and the ride in his car. My critical faculty was dulled; I rejected instinct.

I wanted to be with Alexander and I wanted to show him that he wasn't the only pebble on my beach!

I was lonely and didn't want to be alone.

It all added up to one thing. I quashed my doubts and went to lunch with Ulysses Brett.

His car was an ancient MG sports. The hood was down. I lay low in my seat, put my head back, and watched the trees go by against the sky.

'I'm sleepy,' I said.

'I'm not surprised. I've never seen a girl down lager like you did.'

'Only two half pints,' I yawned. 'It was all that delicious scampi and chips in a basket.'

'I'll wake you.'

'When?'

'When we get there.'

'Where are we going?'

He laughed. 'Relax. Go to sleep. You're safe with me.'

He put his hand on mine where it lay in my lap.

'Don't!' I said, snatching it away from him.

'Sorry!'

'I enjoyed my lunch. And the lagers. Thanks for all of it. But that's all.'

He had taken me to lunch in a pub in Dunster and now he accelerated sharply up the hill. With an effort I took my eyes from the sliding trees and turned my head sideways. His profile gave me no indication of his thoughts.

I said, 'Don't sulk!'

'I'm not.'

'Then what are the black looks about?'

He didn't answer.

'All right! You made a play and I didn't feel like playing.'

I smothered a giggle. Ulysses really was in a huff. His mouth drew tight, his eyes narrowed and his jaw clenched. The speedometer jumped to eighty. I could have used a little tact in my rejection. But why should I? He hadn't used any finesse in his grab at my hand.

A yawn tickled the back of my throat. My sleepless night was catching up on me. I turned my head the other way and rested it in the palm of my hand.

Thoughts slipped through the rising waters of sleep. Ulysses had no sense of humour, he had an overblown idea of his own charm, and as the cousin of the lord of the manor he could even still believe in the *droit de seigneur!* It was a dangerous thing to take oneself too seriously—dangerous, that is, to any one who crossed one's path. Or to anyone who rejected his advances?

I pressed my face into my hand and shut him out of my mind. Why, oh why, wasn't it Alexander at my side?

'Emma!'

I woke with a start.

'We're there.'

I pushed myself up in the seat and stared at the man at my side. He towered over me, filling the little car, blotting out the sky. I was afraid of him.

'Emma . . . wake up.'

He spoke in a low voice, as gentle as a cooing dove, but my fear was not so easily dispelled. I shook my head and ran my fingers through my hair. I smiled at him for I knew that I must never let him see my fear.

'I'm awake now.'

'Hell! You scared me!'

'I scared you?'

'You looked right through me! I felt like a ghost!'

'I'd been dreaming.'

'Of me?'

'It was more like a nightmare.'

'Then it wasn't about me!'

I laughed. My fear went. There was nothing in this red-haired giant of a man to be afraid of.

I looked around and saw that we were in a narrow road with a high hedge on my side and a small churchyard on the other.

'Where are we?'

'Pinkery,' he said. 'Our own, our very own church.'

'You mean the Bretts come here to worship.'

'Those of us who do worship come here. That is when the Vicar comes. Which is every fourth Sunday.'

'And this is what you've brought me to see?'

'Something,' he said, 'that I'm sure will interest you.'

He got out of the car and I, too, got out. My body was stiff. I stretched myself and reached in my handbag for my dark glasses. They are outrageously huge, with brilliants set in the frame. They are flamboyant and I enjoy wearing them.

I put them on and followed Ulysses across the road. Iron railings encircled the overgrown grassland that washed up to the walls of the old stone church. On the right hand side the monumental memorials were lichen-softened, many of them leaning a little, as if wearily falling down to join the long dead people they commemorated.

On the left hand side of the narrow gravel path that led to the church door the grass was cut, the gravestones clean and bright, and there were flowers in vases.

On either side of the gate there were black ornamented metal frames, hollow, about a foot square and higher than my head. On the top of each there were five gold-painted large metal acorns. Along the top of the black metal gate there was a row of gold-painted fleurs-de-lis.

'Someone in the Brett family does a good job of painting,' I said.

He gave me a sharp look. 'Yes,' he said and pushed the gate.

I walked into the shade of a beech tree whose young green leaves were almost fully open. A pair of tall and ragged yew trees stood sentinel on either side of the path, close to the church door. Enclosed on three sides by a solid phalanx of evergreen oaks the air in the churchyard was motionless, hotter than the April day had any right to be.

My father had taught me to know and love ancient buildings. He would have appreciated this small church. I looked at the square Norman tower with the square parapets outlined against the blue of the sky and a sharp pain pierced my heart.

'So now I've seen it.'

I turned on my heel and broke into a run. I had only gone a couple of paces when he was in front of me. I jerked to a standstill. I didn't want to slam into his body, to feel his arms round me again.

'Get out of my way.'

'Not so fast.'

'If you don't move I'll . . .'

'Well? What will you do?'

I flashed a look of venom at him. There were no houses nearby. I could scream and no one would hear.

He looked down at me and there was hard purpose at the back of his eyes. 'I don't still frighten you?'

I stiffened. 'Of course not!

'Then why run away?'

'I'm not running away.'

'Just practising for the hundred yards sprint!'

The sarcasm in his voice was a challenge, but more than this there was my insatiable curiosity. My father was always teasing me that it would be my downfall that one day, like Bluebeard's wife, I would open a forbidden cupboard and come face to face with horror.

But I couldn't stop. I had to go on, to find out what went on behind the façade that people presented to the world, to know what they were really like.

It was evident that a great deal was going on in Ulysses. I looked up into his face. He had his share of the family good looks but his features were coarsened, as if the original mould had blurred. There was a weakness in his mouth that belied the pressure of his gaze. I rejected the instinct to run again and yielded to curiosity.

'Okay,' I said.

A flame of excitement lit in his eyes. It was gone instantly, but I felt the burn of it.

'This way, Emma.'

'This way to the tomb.'

If he heard me he gave no answer. He strode along the path towards the untended section of the churchyard. As he went through the shadow and sunlight his hair dimmed and flared. He didn't hesitate or look back.

I followed, walking slowly and then faster as

he went out of sight. I came round the south end of the church and saw that Ulysses had stopped.

'Come,' he said and held out his hand to me.

I felt a chill so sharp I looked up to see if the sun was veiled. There was not a cloud in the sky. I walked the few steps, ignored his hand and looked down at the gravestone in front of us.

It was very old, a strangely disquieting monument. The base grew out of the ground in a circular hump, and on top of this rose a solid neck. On a level with my eyes there was a large circular headpiece in which at two, four, eight and ten o'clock, there were hollow indentations, like eyes and the corners of a mouth. In the centre there was a rounded protuberant nose. I wanted to look away but I was magnetised by the grey-green, lichen-encrusted face.

'Well?'

I swallowed. 'Interesting.' With an effort I tore my gaze from the grotesque monument. 'If that's all you wanted me to see I don't know why you bothered.'

'Look at the inscription.'

I bent. There were letters concealed in the lichen. Someone had dug them out, not fully, just enough to make them legible. I read.

Emma Jane Woollacott. Born 1756. Died 1775. Age 19.

For a moment it was as if I looked at my own tombstone. The blood in my veins froze and the air was too thick to draw into my lungs.

He said, his voice so low it sounded as if it was in my head, 'I thought you'd find it interesting, Emma Jane Woollacott.'

I was back in the twentieth century. The spring sunshine was warm on my head.

'Interesting? It's . . .'

'Exciting?'

'In a way I suppose it is. But it's a horrifying kind of thrill.'

'Your middle name is Jane?' he asked.

'Of course!' My brightness was surface-thin, a frail skin to cover my disquiet. 'To tell you the truth, one of the reasons I'm here on Exmoor is to go on a hunt for my ancestors. It was my father's dream. One day he would take a sabbatical and we would come here together.'

I stopped short as the weight of my loss fell on me again. There would be no long happy browsing search through the churchyards and parish records in the company of my father. He was dead. As dead as this girl who had lived two hundred years ago.

Ulysses said, 'If it's a family tree you're after I'm glad to help with your namesake.'

I let my gaze fall on the girl's name.

'I feel very strange.'

'Nineteen,' he said. 'The same age.'

'She was alive. She felt the warmth of the sun.'

'And beautiful,' he said. 'Like you are.'

My eyes snapped round at him. 'Do you have a picture of her?'

'No,' he said, laughing, his hair like flame in the sunshine as he laughed, too much I thought for my puny attempt at a joke. He sobered. 'Unless you accept legend as being as good as a painting.'

'So Emma Jane Woollacott is a legend around here.'

'She was a little thing. Like you. The daughter of John Woollacott.'

'Like me,' I echoed, mocking him.

He was trying to reach me, to see through my dark

glasses. I watched his eyelids narrow and his pupils dilate and I was glad that he couldn't see the distrust that was growing with every word he said. For surely there was no kindness behind his persistent likening of me to this dead girl.

'John Woollacott was one of the Brett farmers,' he said.

I dropped him a small mocking curtsey. 'Of course, Master,' I said.

He ignored this. He had gone away, out of his body, and was living the story he told.

'John Woollacott worked Hoar Oak Farm . . .'

He had me now. Before I went to sleep in the derelict farmhouse I had felt something deeper than my ordinary interest and concern for deserted buildings. There had been no little ghost fingers tapping on the wall but there was something in the air, a voice calling from a long way away.

'One bright spring day,' he said, 'Emma told her father she'd be back to milk the cows. She was going out for the day but she wouldn't say where. It was after lunch when she went. She waved to him from the gate. She wore a green dress, the colour of her eyes, and she wore her hair loose, so that it fell in a golden shawl around her shoulders.' He paused. Looked me straight in the eyes and said, 'No one saw her alive again.'

'But you know what happened to her.'

'She was found, weeks later, up on The Chains, beyond Pinkery Pond. Face down in the mud.'

I shuddered. 'What was she doing? She must've known it was dangerous. To walk in the bogs up there?'

'It was the blue light, will-o'-the-wisp enticing her away

from her family to a slow and terrible suffocation as she sank into the morass.'

Suddenly, my mind was free of his. 'Unless,' I said, 'it was *your* ancestor who frightened the poor girl into running away from him!'

CHAPTER FIVE

'OR RUNNING to meet him?'

I looked at him with contempt. 'You Bretts really do have an overrated opinion of your sex appeal!' I turned back to the gravestone. Something was wrong with his story. 'Of course!' I cried, triumphant. 'If she came from Hoar Oak why was she buried at Pinkery Church?'

'She was pregnant.'

'Oh . . . poor Emma.'

'She was going to marry the son of a neighbouring farmer.'

'But your ancestor,' I said, my pity and anger for the long dead girl exploding into the realisation of my own involvement with the Bretts, 'got her pregnant. She committed suicide by walking into the marshes. Or . . .' I stared at him in horror. 'She was running away. She was frightened to her death. I—I hope she haunts you all at Hawkridge Manor!'

'Fascinating!'

'What is?'

'That you know, without me telling you, that the Brett family ghost is your namesake.'

'If it's true,' I mocked.

'Oh, it's true. Ask anyone on the moor. They'll tell you.

I was silent. I had listened to his telling of the legend with mixed feelings. Horror and shock, compassion and anger—Ulysses had awoken all of these reactions in me, but I knew that these were only surface emotions. There was something behind the story, something deeper than the words he said. Something that my curiosity kept niggling at me to unearth.

'Why did you bring me here, Ulysses?'

'To show you the grave of your namesake.'

'And to tell me the legend.'

'I thought you'd be interested to know that your family and mine were closely involved two hundred years ago.'

'I am.' I searched his face but there was nothing. He smiled and hid behind his eyes. 'It's just that I don't like stories with sad endings.'

'Then we must try and give the twentieth century relationship a happy ending.' He looked at his watch. 'Time to go,' he said.

I didn't argue. I turned and began to walk back along the path. The lager had left me with a dull headache. I wanted to be in my cool bedroom in the quiet of Aunt Victoria's impersonal friendship.

Most of all I wanted to get away from Ulysses Brett.

I came quickly round the angle of the church. The shadow of the tower lay thick and dark across the wet grass of the modern half of the churchyard.

I stopped in my tracks.

A woman knelt beside a small white stone. There were fresh narcissi, white and orange-eyed, in the vase. The woman's head was bowed, her face hidden in her hands. She was motionless.

I glanced back at Ulysses. I put my finger to my lips and began to tiptoe along the path.

Behind me, Ulysses gave a loud cough.

I could have hit him. My fists clenched in a rush of anger. I was furious with him.

The woman leaped to her feet and I saw that she was not much older than myself. She wore a simple grey dress, caught into a band around her neck, falling in soft folds to her feet. On her head there was a small grey straw hat with a turned up brim. A grey chiffon scarf was tied around the hat in a knot beneath her chin, the long ends floated softly with her movement and then lay still against her small breasts.

I noted all this with an unconscious part of my attention for in that first moment I saw nothing but her eyes. They were huge, the colour of dark pansies, set wide beneath a high sweet forehead and fringed by thick dark lashes. They were the most beautiful eyes I had ever seen. They were full of despair.

'You . . .' It was the voice of a child.

Ulysses came beside me.

'Emma,' he said and I didn't know if he was announcing the fact or confirming the other girl's recognition. 'This is Deidre.'

'I'm sorry,' I said. 'I didn't mean to intrude.'

Her eyes left mine and flamed at his. 'But *you* did.'

'Now Deidre—'

'You did. I know you did.'

'No more of that,' Ulysses said, so bright it hurt to hear him.

'You knew I'd be here.'

'I'd forgotten.'

'Forgotten!' It was a cry of pain. 'It's a year today! One little year! And you've forgotten!'

'Life has got to go on,' he said, without humour.

'All of you! You've all forgotten! Her eyes blazed. She laughed, mocking and bitter. There were tears in her eyes but they didn't fall. 'So passionate! So male! So—' Her voice broke but she raised her chin and contained the tears. 'So cruel.'

Ulysses was unmoved by her outburst. He took a step towards her and his shadow lay on her face.

'Cruel to be kind,' he said. 'You know what Dr. Hallet said.'

She shrank from him as if he hit her. She shrivelled, her shoulders slumped and her mouth quivered, but still she held back the tears.

'I know what you *say* he said,' she accused.

'He told you, Deidre.' There was a world of weary patience in his voice.

'I don't remember.'

She was shaken. Her gaze left his face and wandered in space. It came at last to me. I gave her a small smile and as much affection as I could put into my look. She seemed to understand. Strength came back into her.

'Emma,' she said. 'Hallo.'

'Hallo, Deidre.'

'Forgive me.'

'There's nothing to forgive.'

'Oh, but there is! They would be angry if they knew how rude I'd been to you. You must come and dine.'

'I'd like that.'

'Today's Wednesday. How about tomorrow?'

'Fine. Is Aunt Victoria included in the invitation?'

'She won't come. She never goes anywhere.' Deidre's eyes rested on mine for a moment, dark and empty. Then, as she moved off the grass and onto the path she said, 'I'll expect you at nine. Now if you'll excuse me I have to get back.'

It was on the tip of my tongue to remind her that the day and time were agreed but that she had omitted to tell me the place. I opened my mouth to speak as Deidre turned away but Ulysses got in first, his voice loud so that a couple of crows flew up out of their insect feast on the grass and fled from him to the topmost branches of an oak.

He said, 'He was with that woman again.'

She tensed. 'You wouldn't take him.'

'I told you, Deidre.'

Deidre laughed again, on a high shrill note that set my scalp prickling.

'You told me!'

'Yes.' His lips snapped on each other.

'What I do is my own affair.'

'Unless it affects the boy.'

A strange look came into the back of Deidre's eyes. Was it fear? Vindictiveness? Sadness? It seemed to me that I saw all these flash through her, and something else, something that I couldn't understand.

'Deidre!' Ulysses shouted at her.

'Yes, Ulysses?' She smiled at him, a smile of sweet innocence.

'You know what I'm saying.'

'You're saying that you want a finger in my pie,' she said, sweetly, innocently, taunting him.

'In this, yes, I do. Mrs. Tamyla's bad for the boy. Always shouting at him.'

'As you are shouting at me?'

A muscle jerked in his jaw as he fought to hold himself in control. 'I have to shout! Listen to me, Deidre.'

'You listen, Ulysses. I'm telling you again. For the last time. Keep your rotten scheming mind off my son.'

'*Your* son?'

'*My* son!'

The blood drained out of his face. They stood, motionless, locked in the fight that was suddenly more violent because they were silent.

'Ulysses,' I said, my voice sharp in the silence.

For answer he made a sudden lunge towards her. I don't know if he would have hit her, for as she moved quickly out of his path, I grabbed at him. In a reflex action his arm jerked out at me and he shook me from him as easily as if I were a small child. I stumbled a little, caught my balance and looked from him to the girl.

Deidre was undisturbed. The smile lay sweetly on her lips. I was startled and a little shocked. There had been nothing in my training, at home or at school and university, to prepare me for such people. It shook me to see that Ulysses, too, was smiling at me.

I knew then that this was only one more in a long series of confrontations. That, if he had hit her, it would have eased some secret stress for each of them.

I knew, too, that for some reason of his own, Ulysses had manoeuvred both Deidre and myself. He wanted her to meet me, and he wanted me to witness the relationship between the two of them.

Now, he came to my side. He put his arm round my waist and held me to him.

'Sorry, Emma,' he said. 'No harm done, I hope.'

'None.' I tried to move, but his arm tightened.

'Take no notice of Deidre and me,' he said, his fingers pressing into my ribs. 'We've known each other since we were in the cradle. The three of us, Alex, Deidre and I.' He laughed and I felt his body shake against mine. 'That's right, isn't it Deidre?'

'I must go.' She looked around her. The power had gone out of her and she was vague and lost.

'I'll drive you.'

'No, thank you, Ulysses.' She was a prim little girl repeating a lesson. 'I would perfer to walk.'

Deidre's eyes looked through me as she turned. She lifted her skirt with a dainty turn of her left wrist and walked quickly away along the path. She was like a Fragonard painting, delicate and ethereal. It was hard to believe that she was a repressed volcano, a dynamo of power, but I had witnessed the strength beneath that sweet exterior and I would never forget it.

Deidre went out through the gate. She didn't look back.

'She's forgotten us,' I said, wonderingly.

'No,' he said. 'Simply obliterated us.'

He dropped his arm from my waist.

'What is it with you and her?'

His eyes were fixed on Deidre's retreating figure. As if he hadn't heard my question he said, 'It's Deidre who put the gold paint on the fleurs-de-lis.'

'You didn't you tell me when I mentioned them.'

'I didn't want to.'

'Don't you ever do anything you don't want to?'

Deidre went out of sight behind the hedge. Her going left an emptiness.

Ulysses said, 'I'll drive you back to Westwater.'

'It's certainly too far for me to walk!' I said drily.

We were outside the gate of Aunt Victoria's cottage when we spoke again.

I got out and slammed the door with unnecessary vehemence.

He grimaced. 'Ouch! That hurt!'

'Sorry. I don't always know my own strength. And thanks for the lunch.' I hesitated. 'And for the conducted tour.'

'I'll be seeing you.'

'I'll look forward to that.'

'To seeing me?'

'All of you. The Brett males have got a certain basic appeal.'

'And where do I rate in the popularity poll?'

I had been talking lightly, making last-minute conversation. Now I saw that he was taking me seriously and I reacted with a nervous toss of my head. My untried flirtatious instinct went clumsily into action.

'Marks out of ten?'

'If you like.'

I took off my dark glasses, put the end of one arm of the frame between my lips and examined him in silence.

'Well, Emma? How do I rate with you?'

'I think,' I said, grinning at him, 'I'll take a leaf out of your book.'

'Which one?'

'The way you didn't tell me when I asked about who painted the fleurs-de-lis.'

He didn't answer immediately. When he finally spoke his voice was low but there was no mistaking the authority behind the words.

'I never,' he said, 'do anything unless . . . until . . . I want to.'

The engine roared as he thrust his foot on the accelerator. If I had had an answer it would have been lost in the explosion of his departure.

I had no answer.

I watched the MG race away past the triangle of village green where a group of children played catch on the grass. I waited until it turned right onto the main road and shot behind the houses. Then, unexpectedly deflated, I walked up the garden path and into the cottage.

On the mat there was a white envelope. I picked it up. My name was on it in large capital letters but there was no address. It had been hand-delivered.

I didn't open it. I was expecting a letter from the solicitor about my father's estate and I saw a couple of letters on the table with the telephone.

They were both for Aunt Victoria. She hadn't opened either.

There was a note for me on a sheet of paper in her neat precise hand.

'Alexander phoned three times since lunch. Meet him in the Crown at six. When you do, remind him not to phone again during the day. I don't know why he did. I told him I don't like being interrupted when I'm working. I'm not a social secretary.'

My heart tripped. Alexander wanted to see me.

I opened the other envelope. The handwriting was a perfect copperplate, the brief note was squarely placed in the centre of the page.

My dear Emma,

I would like to talk to you. May I call upon you

for a cup of china tea at four o'clock? If I do not hear from you to the contrary I will be there.

      Yours in all sincerity, Crispin Brett.

I read it twice and then I began to giggle. I had had my quota of girl friends at school and enjoyed the secrets and the rivalry of the teens, but to be honest, my close relationship with my father had been a barrier between me and adolescent males. They bored me. In return, I saw now, I had probably bored them. In any case, whatever the reason, I had never had a man who was more than superficially interested in me.

Now, suddenly, I was involved with three men.

It was a heady sensation. It was also unnerving. The love I had felt for my father and his love for me had been my security but it left me unsophisticated, ill equipped to deal with the situation. For the first time in my life I felt resentment towards my father. He should have taught me a little cunning. But how could he? A man of simplicity, of frank and openhearted faith, he could only teach me the things he understood.

It was up to me. I was on my own now. I had only my instinct to guide me. It was all of it exciting, flattering, a terrific lift to my sad and lonely ego, but I had to keep an ear open to the warning voice within me, the voice that kept on asking, Why? Alexander, Ulysses and Crispin—what did they want of me?

Crispin Brett was at ease in my Aunt Victoria's small sitting room. He sat back in her wing chair while I sat on the edge of a straight-backed chair and poured his tea.

"Milk or lemon?"

'Lemon, thank you, Emma.'

I passed the cup to him. 'I didn't have time fo fix anything other than biscuits. I only got back at a quarter to four. Will you have one?'

I held out the plate to him but he smiled and shook his head.

'I never eat at teatime, thank you.'

'Nor do I,' I said.

Crispin Brett crossed one elegant leg over the other and seemed in no hurry to tell me why he was here. He spoke of the beautiful day, the delights of summer, even with the tourists, on Exmoor and did I ride, because if I did he would be happy to mount me for a chase with the Devon and Somerset Stag Hunt of which he was a member.

I said it was a beautiful day, I was sure that Exmoor, forgetting the ubiquitous tourists, was superb in summer and no I didn't want to chase a stag. I kept my tone impersonal but I looked at him with new eyes. It was inconceivable that this courteous and charming man should ride to the kill of a stag two or three times a week.

He picked up my thought. 'The hounds don't do the killing,' he said.

'They don't?'

'No. The stag is shot.'

'But you chase it.'

'Deer are destructive animals. Have you seen a field of young wheat after the hinds have feasted overnight?'

'No, I haven't.'

'It's ruined, the farmer's livelihood wiped out in a night.'

I said stubbornly, 'You chase it to its death.'

'The stag doesn't know it's being chased to the death. I've seen a stag, many times, when it knows that hounds have lost the scent, stand still and browse.'

I was silent. Long ago I had gone to a fox hunt with a school friend. Only once. I learned then that men on horseback, out for a chase to the kill, become different people. Men and women who are friends, nice people who are kind to children and dogs, become hard, insensitive. Even their faces change and an ugly look comes into their eyes.

I didn't want to think of this quiet and gentle man caught up in the fever of a blood sport.

I said, 'I'm against it. I'll never change.'

'If you intend to stay with us on Exmoor for any length of time,' he said quietly, 'I think you'll find that you will.'

'Never! I'll be dead myself before I see any good in hunting!'

He looked at me without answering, and I saw myself as he must see me, perched on the edge of the chair, full of anger, lashing him with voice and eyes. I knew that he was right, it was already happening to me. The violence was against the hunt, not for it, but it was in me. And this after only a few words of explanation, not even justification, by this quiet man.

I said, changing the subject, shamed by this unexpected insight into myself, 'What happened to you this morning?'

'That's why I wanted to see you. To apologise for what must seem to you to be extreme rudeness on my part.'

'I was a little surprised.'

'But not too angry to let me ask myself to tea.'

'I'm curious, too.'

'It's really very simple, my dear Emma.'

'Then I must be very stupid, for I don't understand.'
'Ulysses saw you yesterday.'
'He did?'
'You and Alexander. Riding together on Samphire.'
'We didn't see Ulysses.'
'He was up on Hoar Oak Hill.'
I said slowly, thinking this out, trying to visualise the hill on the map, 'He must've followed me from Brendon Two Gates.'
Crispin Brett shook his head. 'There's another way from Hawkridge Manor.'
There was a suppressed excitement in him. I felt it suddenly in the cretonne bright room, like the first sharp frost of autumn.
'There is?' I asked.
'Up past Pinkery Pond.'
I stared at him. 'And over The Chains?'
'Over The Chains.'
'Then he's a brave man!' I grimaced, 'or a very stupid one.'
'Ulysses enjoys a challenge. He's my son.'
There was an imperious glint in his eyes, his old world charm was sharpened by an aggressive lift on the chin. With every word I was learning more about Crispin Brett. I was saddened that my first impression was getting knocked down and that my idealistic image of an English gentleman was proving to have feet of clay.
'I, too,' he said, 'walk over The Chains.'
'Bully for both of you!' I clapped my hand to my mouth. 'Oh! I'm sorry! That was rude of me. I can only say that in the last twenty-four hours so much has happened that I am a little off balance. And confused.'
'It is understandable.' He was back to his courteous

self. 'I will remove one confusion for you, Emma. Ulysses saw you. He wanted to get to know you. I appreciate the company of a lovely young girl like yourself but I will not be a middle-aged swain! Besides, as I already said, he is my son. It isn't easy for Ulysses, living at Hawkridge Manor, in the house of his cousin. So I do what I can for him. When he said he would like to take you to the Festival of The Hobby Horse I said I would stand down in favour of him.'

I had listened to the spate of words, trying to sort out my own reaction. It was all talk of 'Ulysses, my son,' but I felt that there was something else. The humility, the readiness to 'stand down' didn't go with the aggression, the suppressed excitement, I had felt only a moment ago.

'Emma,' he said.

I started. I looked into his face and I felt foolish. I saw nothing more than a patient and kindly middle-aged man, sitting forward on his chair in his concern for myself.

'I was thinking. I still don't understand why Ulysses didn't come and fetch me this morning.'

'That is more difficult to explain.'

'Try.'

'Ulysses and I are the Brett poor relations.'

'Ah!'

'We live at Hawkridge by the generosity of the lord of the manor.'

'Alexander,' I said.

'He's a man of high principles. I wouldn't want you to think, not for a moment, that I am saying a word against him.'

But you hate his guts! I pressed my lips tightly together in panic that I had spoken aloud. I hadn't. Crispin Brett was rising to his feet with an easy grace.

I stood, too. 'Are you going?'

'I've taken up too much of your time and bored you with my tale of poverty.'

'It can't be easy,' I said, going with him to the door.

'But it is certainly bad manners to speak of it.' He opened the door and bowed me through. 'I will not burden you again with the problems of myself and my son.' He moved quickly across the hall and opened the front door. He stood still and turned to me and took my hand in his. 'You're a kind and lovely girl, Emma,' he said. 'And I'm old enough to be your father so may I plead privilege and give you a piece of advice.'

'So long as you don't expect me to follow it!'

'Naturally not. You are young. The young go their own way.'

'Still,' I said. 'Give it to me. Who knows? Maybe I'm old enough to understand that you could know something I should think about.'

He bent his head, lifted my hand, and his lips were warm on the back of my hand. He raised his head and looked straight into my eyes. 'Emma,' he began. 'You should think about if you should stay—'

My Aunt Victoria's voice was a knife thrown between us.

'Why, Crispin! I didn't know you were here. Emma, you should have fetched me.'

'I'm sorry, Aunt Victoria. From your note I thought you didn't want to be disturbed.'

'Silly girl! I'll always be disturbed for a friend. And Crispin is an old and true friend.'

Her gaze fell on our clasped hands. I snatched mine

back to my side and suddenly I had had enough.

'If you'll excuse me,' I said, 'I'll clear the tea things.'

I went back into the sitting room. I picked up the tray and hurried through the hall. They had gone. I saw them by the gate, heads close, talking. I hurried into the kitchen. The electric clock on the wall told me that it was fourteen minutes to six. If anyone ever said to me again that life in the country was slow or dull I would laugh and laugh.

I left the tray on the table. It would have to wait until later.

I only had thirteen minutes to get myself as beautiful as I could for Alexander.

CHAPTER SIX

I saw him at once.

He was at the far end of the pub. The lighting was dim, there were already about twenty customers leaning against the bar, seated at low tables against the walls, but my eyes went to him as if I knew where he would be. As if this wasn't the first time we had met in The Crown at Exbury. As if we had met at the table in the corner beyond the plum-coloured curtains that framed the small window not once but many times before.

I paused in the entrance. He saw me. He smiled at me and the distance that separated us grew smaller.

I walked to him. He stood up and motioned me to sit on the seat against the wall. I waited for the sound of his voice, for the contact of words to confirm my feeling of intimacy.

Alexander said, 'What'll it be?'

My foolish heart heard his mundane enquiry as if he opened the gates to heaven itself. 'Lager.' I said.

'Funny!'

'Am I?'

'I thought you'd ask for our local cider. Being a Woollacott.'

An unsuspected ancestral taste bud stirred in sleep. 'Of course. You're right. That's exactly what I'd like.'

He walked across the pub. I clung to him with my eyes. His body was as I remembered it, tall, broad-shouldered, narrow-hipped. The way he walked was as great a delight as the inner eye had pictured it. I moved impatiently, shifting on the hard seat. I wanted him to come back. I wanted to see his face, to know again the feeling of unity.

Alexander came back but he didn't look at me. He put the glass mugs on the table. He sat on the chair on the other side of the table and offered me an open cigarette case. I looked at it. It was gold. There was an inscription, half-concealed by cigarettes so that I couldn't read the words, but I could feel the chill of his change of mood.

'No thanks,' I said. 'I don't smoke.'

'Very sensible.'

He took a cigarette for himself, snapped the case and put it on the table. He lit his cigarette with a match.

'I claim no credit. I don't like it.'

'Don't like what?'

'Smoking.'

I sneaked a look at his face and wished that I hadn't. He was a stranger. I took up my glass and drank the cider fast. It was cool and it had a tang that woke all of those ancestral taste buds.

'It's delicious,' I said.

'I knew you'd like it.'

I raised my eyebrows at him. 'Knew?'

For a simple beat of my hopeful heart I thought we were together again.

Alexander said, 'There's nothing deep in my guessing. Your Aunt Victoria is an addict.'

The shutter was fully, firmly, down between us. 'Like aunt, like niece,' I said and drained my mug. 'I'd like another, please, Alexander.'

'That's not like Aunt.'

'Like myself.'

'She knows better.'

'There's a lot I have to learn.'

'This cider's a potent brew.'

'Then it's just what I need.'

'Emma.'

I stood up. 'I'll get my own.'

'Oh . . . sit down!'

He picked up the glass mug and strode away from me. Every line of his back was stiff. I couldn't believe that this was the same back I had watched with such yearning only a few minutes before. He had been relaxed and now he was tense, and I had done it to him. What else could I have done? How did he expect me to react to his incomprehensible changes of mood?

He was coming back.

As he sat down, I said, 'Thanks.'

'Drink this one slowly.'

I made conversation. 'I've washed your shirt but I haven't had time to iron it.'

'I told you not to trouble.'

'It's no trouble.' I went straight on, the words bursting out of me. 'Alexander, what's wrong?'

'Nothing's wrong.'

'Oh, yes it is! Everything's wrong! Is it something *I* said?'

'No.'

'Something I've done?'

'No.'

'Left undone?'

He took a deep drag on the cigarette and stabbed it in the ashtray. 'It's nothing to do with you, Emma.'

'Then why take it out on me?'

He lifted his head in the middle of taking another cigarette and stared at me.

'I'm sorry,' he said, and looked down again, busy with the flaring match. 'I don't mean to.'

He stopped short. The sentence didn't seem finished. But I had already got myself into a state of unnerved doubt by reading things into him that he hadn't said. I wouldn't do it again, I would have a straight answer from him.

'What do you mean?' I asked.

'It's difficult.'

'It was you,' I pointed out, 'who suggested this meeting.'

'I had to see you.'

My heart leaped again. I took another drink. If this went on, if I had to keep drinking as a cover-up, I would very soon be under the table. I slammed the mug down. To my discomfort a dollop of cider slopped over the top and fell in a pale gold pool on the table.

'Well,' I said, 'here I am. You can see me if you lift your head.'

'You're very sharp today, Emma.'

The sadness in him cut me deeply. 'You've changed, too.'

'Yesterday was a day out of time. It happened. It'll always be there. You will always be there. Every time I walk in the door at Kithore I'll see you.'

He was silent. I was most acutely aware of him. I started down into the cider. I couldn't look at him. He was saying he words I wanted to hear but there was something wrong with his voice. It wasn't the tone of a man who remembered happy, enchanted hours. He spoke coldly. No, even that was too strong an evaluation of his emotion. He spoke *coolly*. Not so much as if he disciplined himself, as if there was only a small passion to remember, as if he felt he must let me down gently.

My eyes flew to his. 'You don't have to be kind to me.'

He looked at me and said, like a whisper, 'I would be kind to you.' And immediately, as if he had said more than he should, he looked down at the slopped cider. 'Grow a skin, Emma. There's little enough kindness around.'

'That's up to us.'

'Us?'

'I mean to collective us.'

'Of course.'

We relapsed again into an uneasy silence. I held my mug in both hands and gazed down into the pale gold cider as if it was a crystal ball. No beautiful future appeared, no handsome stranger. How could it? He was here, sitting at the other side of the table, not looking at me. It seemed as if he had closed the door on the future with his warning to grow a protective covering.

Our silence was oppressive. I must say something now or it would get so heavy that we would never struggle up out of it again.

I said lightly, 'The strangest thing happened to me on the way to the pub.'

My attempt at humour got through to him. He relaxed back in his chair and asked, 'And what was this strange thing that happened to you on the way to the pub?'

'Well, not exactly on the way here. It was this afternoon. There was this girl in the churchyard. She asked me to dinner tomorrow at eight. The strange thing is that she forgot to tell me where.'

It was only a small part of the story but I told it briefly and fast for I wanted to know his reaction.

It exceeded anything that I had hoped. Or feared.

He thrust back his chair and stood up. 'Let's get out of here.'

I followed Alexander. It didn't even occur to me that I had a choice.

He drove to Dunkery Gate. He parked the car and we got out. The beacon reared against a dark cloudy sky but behind us it was blue with little white sheep clouds playing tag.

'Can you walk?'

'As well as you!'

I had put on my yellow sandals with three-inch heels to meet him at The Crown. They were ridiculous footwear for the climb but I didn't hesitate. I felt a deep unhappiness in him. If I felt it would help him, I would crawl up to Dunkery Beacon on my hands and knees, and if this was a brash and foolish assertion to make, even within myself, it was how I felt.

So I stumbled and lurched up the steep stony hard earth path in his wake. Halfway up, he turned and waited for me to reach him. He took my hand in his, and hand in hand we went on up the hill.

It was a beautiful evening and there had been a couple of cars in the park but if there were people on Dunkery they moved outside the circle of my consciousness.

I saw the butterflies, as frail as tissue-paper, no longer

than my little fingernail. They danced and fluttered over the heather, as far as the eye could see. My heart danced and fluttered with them for Alexander's hand held mine.

We came, at last, to the top of the hill and stood beside the high stone beacon. Great banks of cloud rolled over the wide sky, waves of sunlight and shadow flowed beneath them, up and down the hills and valleys, over the flat grey surface of the Bristol Channel.

Alexander dropped my hand and the wind shot through me. Goose pimples broke out on my neck above the scooped blouse and I began to shiver. He was standing a little in front of me, his head lifted, the wind blowing his hair straight back from his face. I felt shut out. I tried to think of something to say but this was not the moment for social chat and I was nervous of anything personal.

And then, without a word he took off his jacket and put it round me. It was warm with the heat of his body. I slid my arms into the sleeves and hugged it close to me. 'It's getting to be a habit,' I laughed, 'borrowing your clothes. Are you all right?'

'Let's go down over Dunkery Hill. It's a bit sheltered. And,' he smiled, briefly, 'in case you've got me wrong, I'm not cold. There are things I have to say to you. I don't find words easy. It'll help if we walk.'

We walked. This path was easier, a gentle slope with smaller, fewer stones, and little pools, miniature mirrors of the blue sky that spread out to the hills on the southern horizon. Light sparkled against my eyes from the water.

I said, 'A sun in every puddle.'

Alexander went straight on as if he hadn't heard. 'This

morning I decided it would be best for everyone concerned if I bowed out.'

'So you sent Crispin in your place.'

'He was agreeable.'

'And Ulysses? Did he hear your shout?'

'Is it important?'

'I just wanted to get things straight for the record.'

'No,' he said. 'He didn't hear me. At any rate he didn't answer. It didn't matter. I went to Dunster. I didn't intend to see you again.'

'So what changed your mind?'

He said, 'I suppose she told you.'

'The girl in the churchyard?' I countered but it was a last-ditch evasion. I knew what he was going to say.

'Did she?'

'She told me a number of things. Which particular . . .'

He broke in. 'I should've told you yesterday.'

I wouldn't say it. So long as the words were unspoken I could continue in my dream. 'Let's just enjoy our walk, Alexander.'

But he wouldn't let me dream. 'Deidre is my wife,' he said.

I swallowed. It was foolish to feel so lonely. I had only known Alexander Brett for a day and a half. He couldn't be so important to me, but it was as if his words cut my life in half. At the same time I was aware of relief. In the moment when I first saw the girl, instinct had told me who she was. My folly lay in my stubborn refusal to admit what I already knew.

He stopped. 'Oh God!' He turned to me. 'I forgot.'

The wind whispered the cry from his lips but the pain in him seemed to go on and on so that I had to hug his jacket even closer around me to stop myself from throwing my arms around him and holding him close and safe from the grief that burned within him.

There was nothing I could do. I said, because I couldn't deny it for him, 'Yes, Alexander. You forgot.'

He looked through me. 'Our little daughter,' he said. 'She only lived for eleven months.'

'And Jason,' I asked. 'Is he yours?'

His eyes cleared and his look pierced me. 'Jason wasn't with her.'

'No. But she talked about him.'

'What did she say about Jason?'

'Nothing much.'

'What?'

I shifted beneath the icy probing of his eyes. 'Just chat about him going to see the Hobby Horse. It was a bit embarrassing. She and Ulysses . . .'

'Ulysses!'

'It was Ulysses who took me to Pinkery Church,' I explained.

'To see the grave of my ancestor,' I said, talking crisply because I didn't understand and because with every word I was further away from him.

'But you were with Crispin.'

'I changed partners,' I said brightly.

'And why shouldn't you?'

He was gone again. His voice and eyes were bitter, mocking, but whether his mockery was directed against me or himself I couldn't be sure.

'As a matter of fact,' I said, 'I wished I hadn't gone. It was embarrassing. Ulysses and Deidre had a nasty argument about Jason.'

He turned from me and strode down the hill. I had to break into a run to keep up with him.

'Alexander! Wait.'

He stopped and turned. As I came to him he said, 'Quarrels! Fights! With Jason at the heart of it! One day I'll . . .'

His lips drew tight on the unfinished sentence. Dark streaks of hair whipped across his forehead. His eyes were black as darkness.

'Jason is your son,' I said, foolishly stating the obvious.

'Yes.'

'I saw him.'

'You did?'

'At the Hobby Horse. We had quite a chat. He told me he's learning to play the drum.'

I succeeded. The bitterness went out of him. 'That's my Jason.' There was pride and laughter in his voice. 'That's my boy! Anything to make a noise, to make the rest of us aware of him!'

'We all like to be heard,' I said.

He turned and began to talk along the path again.

'Sometimes the general clamour is so loud it's difficult to get across to . . . anyone.'

I walked at his side. 'Try me.'

It could have been the wind that kept my words from his ears, or it could have been that I, too, failed to reach him across the general clamour of his involvements. Certainly, he didn't answer me, not directly.

He said, 'I have responsibilities.'

It was quiet, emotionless, final.

We came to the end of the path and I stepped off at his side onto the road. The sun was lowering to the far hills, its rays washing over the valley in a flood of golden light. The shadow of a tree was a purple pool on the road.

I waded through it and came out into the warm glow again.

I said, 'I wanted to see Tarr Steps before I went back to London.'

'You're not leaving?'

'I think I should.'

'Because of what I said?'

'It's what you meant me to understand. Isn't it?'

'Of course,' he said, not answering, 'if you have commitments...'

'Some. They're not urgent.'

'Or if you want to leave.'

'Do you,' I asked, weighing each word, 'want me to go?'

'I have no right.'

'Oh, Alexander!' I laughed briefly. 'Can't you ever give a straight answer!'

'I can't add you to my...'

I broke in. 'Stop it!'

'Stop what?'

'Look at me!' I put my hand on his arm and gripped the cold shirt and pressed my fingers into his flesh. 'I'm myself! Me! Emma Jane Woollacott! You have no responsibility to me! Nor I to you! So stop talking as if we're indulging in an earth-shattering relationship and answer my question with a plain yes or no. Do you want me to go?'

He looked at me a long time. I searched his eyes but I couldn't tell what he was thinking. I waited, scarcely breathing. I had never spoken like this to any other human being and I was startled by my own reckless behaviour.

I began to shake. He could say *something*. He *should*

say something. I had gone way out on a limb and there was no way back. No way. Not without his help. The trembling increased and I clung to his arm, for now I could fall without its support.

'No.'

I stared at him. 'No?' I echoed.

'Yes.'

'Yes, you mean no?'

He began to laugh. He unfastened my fingers from his arm and held them in his hand.

'Oh, Emma' he laughed. 'You're crazy!'

His laughter infected me. 'The whole world's mad,' I said. 'Except thee and me. And even thee's a bit mad.'

He looked at his watch. 'There's time,' he said. 'We can finish our cider before I go back to Hawkridge for dinner.' He stopped laughing and said, his eyes on mine, 'Tomorrow you'll be dining in my house.'

CHAPTER SEVEN

'HAWKRIDGE MANOR,' Aunt Victoria told me, is on the road to Challacombe. You go through Simonsbath to Goat Hill. There's a sharp left-hand bend in the road. You can't miss it. Go through the gate on the right.'

'You don't mind?' I asked as she stopped.

'Being left behind? Or if you go?'

'Both.'

'No. And yes.'

'You don't approve of the Brett family.'

'Emma,' Aunt Victoria said in a gruff voice that defied contact, 'your father was a romantic. You think I live here like a hermit. Maybe I do, but I'm still more worldly than your father ever was in his suburban flat and his idealistic hope of teaching art to all and sundry.'

We were in her kitchen. I had spent the day touring and walking. I had been to Tarr Steps and walked along the bank of the River Barle to Withypool and back. I was relaxed and hungry. I was looking forward to a good dinner, to seeing Alexander in the bosom of his family, and discovering more about him and his relationship with Deidre.

HAWKRIDGE

I watched my aunt cut bread and put it on a plain white plate. Bread, cheese, fruit and coffee were to be her evening meal. Aunt Victoria might not be a hermit but she was certainly an ascetic.

She was also giving me a brief character outline of the Bretts of Hawkridge Manor.

'Crispin,' she said, brusque and impersonal, 'is a charmer.' She shot a glance at me from beneath lowered brows. 'Oh, yes, Emma! There was a time when I considered marrying Crispin. Don't be fooled. Take a tip from me. Don't listen to the voice of the charmer. Beneath the surface there's an iron purpose.'

She went into the pantry. I waited until she came back with a wooden bowl piled with oranges and apples in one hand and a bottle of milk in the other. As she plunked them down on the table I said, 'What "iron purpose" can Crispin have?'

Aunt Victoria ignored my question. 'Ulysses,' she said 'is a chip off the old block.'

'All charm and iron?' I mocked.

'You're a fool, Emma. Just like your father. You believe that the world is populated by decent Christian folk. It isn't. Man*kind* is a misnomer. The sheep on the moor, the fox in his lair, *they* are kindly. Humans? Not on your life!'

She stomped off again, returning in a moment to slam down the butter still in its paper and a lump of cheddar cheese that was actually on a plate.

"Ulysses is a hedonist, a hunter of stags and women.' Her quick eye caught my antagonism. 'The image attracts you, does it?'

'I can't see that it's so wicked to love women.'

'Who said love?'

'Even to desire a woman isn't evil.'

'I know it's the custom of young people today to treat physical passion between a man and a woman as no more than an acrobatic entertainment.'

'I didn't say that!'

'But it's what you mean.'

'No. You're wrong, Aunt Victoria. I think it is vital, essential, to love a man. And to know that he loves me.'

'Then give a wide berth to Ulysses. I don't hold it against him that he's got the natural predatory instincts of the young male. What makes him dangerous is his absolute self-esteem. He was spoiled as a small boy. In a misguided attempt to compensate for the loss of his mother, and for the fact that he was the cousin and not the heir, everyone bent over backwards to give to Ulysses Brett. The result is simple. Ulysses sees himself as the centre of a world that owes him a living.'

'And Alexander?'

'Alexander is Lord of the Manor.'

'Is that a mark for or against him?'

Aunt Victoria leaned on the back of a high wooden chair and looked at me hard. 'There have been Bretts at Pinkery for 700 years. In the thirteenth century a Brett was Warden of Exmoor, royally appointed to look after the King's interests in matters of pasturage and boundaries and to keep the royal table supplied with venison. For all these duties he was paid an annual fee of £11.92. Alexander makes a bit more than this today!' She allowed herself a brief smile. 'His job is confined to the sheep and cattle on Pinkery and to his antique shops in Minehead and Duster. And to assuring the continuation of the line. It was lucky, since he had to marry the girl, that the child turned out to be a boy.'

'You mean Deidre was pregnant?'

'Heavens above! What else could I mean?'

I said, keeping my voice light, hiding my thoughts behind lowered eyelids. 'Shotgun weddings are long out of fashion.'

I am an incompetent actress. Aunt Victoria picked up my thoughts.

'I'm warning you about Alexander.'

'You warned *him* about *me*.

Aunt Victoria tossed her head. 'I did. I told him that my niece is not for the amusement of himself or his uncle or his cousin.'

I flushed. 'You had no right to interfere in my life.'

'Hoity-toity, miss! I have every right as your only living relative. Especially when you decide to visit me for the first time in your nineteen years.' She was suddenly angry with me. 'It is *you*, Emma, who is interfering with *my* life.'

I drew myself up and faced her with what I hoped was a dignified regret. 'I'm sorry, Aunt Victoria, if I'm a nuisance.' I felt lonely and worried and angry, all at once.

'Come, girl, don't get up on your high horse. And, Emma, another thing.'

'Yes, Aunt?' I was aggressively submissive.

'Listen to me. There was a rumour. When it gets about that you're going around with the Bretts from Hawkridge Manor, someone will tell you. It's best you hear it from me.'

'Rumour!' I snapped. 'I never listen to rumour and gossip.'

'Then you'd better start now,' she said drily.

'Okay! Let's dish the dirt!'

I heard what she said. Her voice was clear, the words

were simple, and there was no possible way I could change their meaning.

In the silence when she finished there was the rising shriek of the boiling kettle. Neither of us moved. We looked at each other across the bright yellow table and the kettle went on screaming.

'I had to tell you, Emma.'

'Oh, no you didn't! You wanted to tell me!'

'That's unfair!'

'And those people, whoever they are, those village gossips. They are fair?'

'Some of those people are my friends, Emma.'

'Then they're no friends of mine!'

She looked at me a moment without speaking. The kettle shrieked. 'You'll be late for dinner,' she said. 'You'd better go.'

'Oh, I'm going!' I swung on my heel. In the doorway I turned and threw my last bolt. 'Don't wait up for me. I may never come out alive from dining at Hawkridge Manor!'

I slammed the door of the cottage and a moment later, the door of my car. Neither outburst did anything to relieve my disquiet.

The day had deteriorated as much as my relationship with my Aunt Victoria. There had been angry words inside and there were storm clouds overhead. As I drove out onto the main road I switched on my headlamps for it was already too dark to see.

I drove fast across the moor but I couldn't drive fast enough to outdistance the terrible thing that she had said. It was, of course, impossible. She had admitted to a broken relationship with Crispin. She lived alone with her everlasting chipping at slabs of stone or marble.

These things could have grown into a canker. Her brooding could have turned into a festering enmity against all the Bretts.

How about myself? In my state of emotional turmoil, could I disentangle truth from jealous fantasy?

I didn't know him well. I didn't know him at all. He hadn't exactly lied to me but nor had he been exactly honest. He was, even on so brief an acquaintance, a complicated man. Or was it that the outside pressures forced him to be complex and devious?

I had come to the turn off the main road but I had resolved none of my thoughts. The beam of my headlights flashed across white gates, over a small stream, and back onto a narrow road that rose slowly before me.

I drove in third gear, trying to settle my thoughts, but they raced as fast as the wind-driven clouds. I didn't understand that I was already past the point of no return. I was already more than half in love with Alexander Brett and my Aunt Victoria's revelation that he had 'had to marry' Deidre had the opposite effect from the one she thought she would achieve, for I reasoned that in this case it was possible that he had never felt deeply for his wife.

And that, I thought wryly, made him one of Aunt Victoria's passion-without-love men! I didn't care. I wanted the affair between Alexander and Deidre to have been no more than a summer's night hot-blooded youth relationship that had resulted in pregnancy and marriage.

This way, Alexander had never been emotionally committed. He was free to fall in love with me.

And where did that lead us?

I had no time to answer this unanswerable question. The beam of my lights swung over grassland and back onto the road as it swung to the right. At that moment the wind tore a rift in the black racing sky and I saw his house.

Hawkridge Manor was above me on a plateau. In the eerie light it seemed suspended between the dark grassland of the sloping hill below and the darker mass of trees that enclosed it on the rising hill at the rear, a white ghost of a house floating in space.

I drove slowly up the last steep slope and stopped in the circular drive. I saw now that the house was firmly rooted in the earth. Someone had planted hydrangeas that would be a bank of colour in the summer but which now, in the green light of the storm, writhed along the foot of the building like a forest of serpents.

I doused the engine and cast the fantasies from my head. I looked again, examining Alexander's house with the affectionate and critical eyes of my Father.

Hawkridge Manor was an austere building. My critical sense was delighted by the smooth square lines, by the narrow oblong windows and a roof line that cut a horizontal line against the sky. Later I was to see that a wing of red brick, set back from the main building, had been added by Alexander's grandfather. Now I saw only the white front of the original manor house and the flight of shallow steps leading up to a circular Doric porch, and between the white pillars, a pool of shadow so dark that I could only glimpse the great front door.

I switched off my headlamps and got out of the car. There was no sign of welcome. No evidence that anyone lived in Hawkridge Manor. The windows were closed and no light shone through them. The picture of Alexander Brett waiting for me at the open door of his manor house, a fire of huge logs flaming in the immense fireplace in the hall beyond him, faded for ever.

I braced my shoulders. I was hungry. I like to eat at seven and it was already a quarter past nine. For the second time that evening I slammed the door of my car as if I tried to wake the dead, or at least to make the living aware of my existence.

I walked a few paces. I reached the flight of steps. The space in the clouds closed and I was in darkness. I stopped, balancing uneasily on the first step, waiting for my eyes to adjust. And then, as if at a signal, the great door at the top of the steps deep in the cave of the porch began to move. I couldn't see it but I knew that it was swinging on its hinges, slowly, noiselessly, opening into a further black velvet cavern.

Suddenly I was angry. I fumbled for the next step and called, 'What kind of game is this?'

Light hit me, blazing down from a point high up beneath the curve of the porch above the door, a white light that burned my dark-accustomed eyes. I put up my hand and steadied myself on the second step. Shading my eyes with my hand I peered upwards.

Somewhere beyond the light, against the thick darkness of the hall, I saw a small shimmering figure.

'Emma!' While I caught my breath she came down the steps in a swift run. 'You're here!' Her voice was soft, a little breathless, as if she had played a childish prank and expected a rebuff. She reached me. Her arms went round me and a warm fragrant cheek pressed against mine. 'Oh, Emma! I'm so happy to see you.'

Before I could answer, Alexander's voice came from the darkness beyond the beam of the spotlight.

'What the hell's going on?'

Light filled the interior of the house. My instant impression was of the warmth of a rust-coloured carpet led along a short passage to the wide square hall. I saw Ulysses standing by the front door, smiling. I saw Crispin at the foot of the wide staircase that ended on the right in the centre of the hall. He held a torch in his hand, the light still on. He looked at me, smiling.

I saw Alexander, his hand raised to the switch on the wall opposite the staircase. My Aunt Victoria's Lord of the Manor was not smiling.

'Deidre,' he said, 'What the devil are you playing at?'

She didn't answer. She twisted to face the house but she kept her arm around my waist. I do not like casual feminine embraces and I was on the point of extricating myself when she leaned her face against mine and whispered, her breath warm and sweet, 'Look at him, Emma! Isn't he beautiful?'

I looked at the three of them. Ulysses wore a velvet suit the colour of autumn leaves, the black polo-neck of the silk jersey accentuating the whiteness of his skin. Crispin was immaculate in black tie, white shirt, black dinner suit. Alexander wore a suit in midnight blue with braded reveres, a white shirt with a frilled cente strip, and a midnight blue bow tie.

'The Brett males,' I murmured in appreciation. 'All of them beautiful.'

'But only one of them is a murderer.'

I froze. 'Is that meant to be funny, Deidre?'

'Laugh if it helps.'

I looked from Ulysses to Crispin to Alexander. The tableau was breaking up. They were moving, Ulysses onto the porch, Crispin across the hall, Alexander towards the door. Deidre wasn't joking. Nor had Aunt Victoria laughed. Not Alexander, it couldn't be Alexander.

I asked, my voice as cold as my face, 'Which one?'

And then Deidre laughed. Her cheek soft and warm and scented against mine she whispered, 'You tell me!'

Ulysses reached us. 'Tell you what, Deidre?'

'Secrets,' she said, tucking her arm through mine. 'Girl talk . . . not for masculine ears!'

Alexander stood in the doorway of his house. The light poured down on him. His eyes were black in the shadow of the bones of his forehead.

He said, 'Hallo, Emma.'

'Hallo, Alexander,' I said.

I tried then to disentangle myself but Deidre's hold tightened so that we mounted the steps together.

'Look at him,' Deidre chanted. 'Furious with me!'

'It was a silly trick,' he said.

'I was only testing the new light.'

Ulysses said, 'Actually, it was my idea.'

'You should test it on each other, not on our guest.'

Deidre gave my arm a quick squeeze and, lifting her skirt, ran the last few steps and arranged herself at the side of her husband. Her dress was in silver lamé, body-clinging, a sophisticated style that made her look like a little girl dressed up in her mother's clothes. There was a feverish excitement in her eyes.

She held out her hand so that it drooped from the angle of her wrist. A solitaire diamond topped the wedding ring, covered the first joint of her finger, caught the light and sent it flashing.

'Good evening, Miss Woollacott,' she said, her voice high, oozing with unctuous superficial charm. 'Do please come into our humble abode.'

Alexander took her hand down from its height of mocking welcome. I reached the platform of the top step and saw that his face was white but he spoke to her gently. 'A bit exaggerated, but I'm sure that Emma prefers this welcome to being blinded by a searchlight meant for prowlers.'

They waited for my answer. 'To be honest...' I began.

'Must be honest!' Deidre interrupted.

I looked at their hands clasped between them, and looked quickly up again to smile at her.

'To be honest,' I said, 'I'm dying for a drink.'

CHAPTER EIGHT

'CHAMPAGNE!'

Deidre released his hand. Singing 'The Blue Danube' in a sweet and true soprano, she held out her arms to an imaginary partner and circled slowly though the hall.

'Alexander's opening a bottle of his special vintage, specially for you, Emma. Champagne goes with waltzing. Alexander?'

I caught the glance she threw at Alexander as she circled in front of him. It was a challenging provocative look to which Alexander said, 'Not now, Deidre.'

'Now! Now!'

'Calm down.'

She tossed her head. 'I don't want to calm down!' She circled on round the hall, a whirling shimmering doll that had been wound up and couldn't stop. 'I want to dance! If you're going on with your sulks there're others who will dance with me.'

Ulysses went quickly past me. 'I will, for one.'

She gave him a withering look. 'You can't waltz!' she scoffed and stopped in front of Crispin. She dropped him a curtsey. Looking up at him, her face as bright as a child looking up at a Christmas tree, she said, 'Please, Crispin, dance with me!'

Alexander said, 'Deidre,' in a tone that was like the retort of a gun. 'Emma is in our house at your invitation.'

She was contrite. Crispin held out his hand to her but she didn't see it. She was up on her feet, running towards me with her quick light movements.

'Of course she is! How naughty of me! Come with me, Emma. I'll take care of you.'

I can take care of myself, I thought but something in her eyes, something in Alexander's taut face, kept me quiet.

'Thanks, Deidre,' I said and was rewarded by a slight easing of Alexander's tight-lipped control as I followed her.

'This is the white drawing room,' she said. She waved her left hand and the diamond sparkled. 'Those doors open into the ante room and beyond that there are more sliding doors into the morning room. One day we'll have a grand ball and open all the doors and have a string orchestra in the hall and dance till dawn. That is, if I can persuade my husband to come out of his grumps!'

For myself, I was satisfied with the drawing room as it was. A twelve-branch chandelier in the centre of the ceiling reflected in a gilt-edged mirror that reached from the green marble mantelpiece to the ceiling and gave the room an extra dimension. My anticipated log fire blazed merrily in the huge open grate. The carpet was patterned in cerise and gold, the curtains of cerise brocade and the main furniture in gold and white stripes. Small ornate gilt chairs, three upholstered in gold and one in cerise stood around the room. There were oil paintings on the walls that I wished I had time to examine.

I looked round for Alexander. He was beside a small table against the far wall, preoccupied with the opening of the bottle of champagne. At his side Crispin was watching me. He gave me an appreciative smile but I felt that if I had turned a moment sooner I would have seen a different reaction.

The cork popped.

Deidre clapped her hands. 'Oh, well done, Alex!'

Crispin held the glass for the frothing champagne.

Ulysses smiled round at everyone from his straddle-legged place in front of the fire.

I looked away from him. He had usurped Alexander's position. At this, I checked myself. Hawkridge, I told myself severely, is Ulysses' home, too. I must stop my foolhardy castle-in-the-air building. It could do no one any good and it would surely do me harm.

'Daydreaming, Emma?'

I started. Crispin stood in front of me, between me and Ulysses. I blushed. 'It's such a lovely room,' I said, but I saw in his eyes that he read my thoughts.

'Your champagne.'

The glass was cool. 'Thank you, Crispin.'

'Cigarette?'

He offered me an open silver box. I took a cigarette and he lit it for me with a large silver lighter that he picked up from the table.

'You and Alexander have something in common,' he said.

'I doubt that!'

'Don't be alarmed.'

'I'm not!'

'You blushed.'

'Ah,' I said, gathering my wits together, aware of a subtle pressure of the mind beneath his old world charm. 'I plead guilty.'

'It is a delight to see.'

'But not to feel. I'm sorry to say that it came because I yielded to the deadliest of the seven sins.'

They were all listening now. Their glasses in their hands they waited, but if it was only for me or if it was something deeper I couldn't tell.

Crispin said, forestalling Alexander's move, 'My dear Emma, you'll never make me believe that you could covet your neighbour's ox or ass or husband.'

I said quickly, hiding my shock beneath a light banter. 'You're right, Crispin. I'm not a covetress, if there is such a word. But I love beautiful works of art. All this,' I waved my hand round the room, 'is a far cry from a two-bed flat in Richmond. My deadly sin is envy.'

It was then that I turned and looked at Ulysses. His eyes were waiting for me The contact held briefly, but if I had hoped to learn anything Ulysses was giving nothing away. His gaze was the melting brown-eyed look of a spaniel as he raised his glass to me in a silent toast.

'Not many people,' Crispin said, 'would have the courage to admit their faults in open session.'

Deidre came darting to my side. 'Let's play the truth game!'

She was scintillating, vitally alive. I smiled at her and was angry with Alexander as he said, 'We're not schoolgirls, Deidre.'

She was unrepressed. 'Let your hair down for once, darling. Let's all have fun.'

I said, standing at her side so that we faced the three men, 'As you asked me Crispin, let's begin with you.'

He moved across the hearth in front of Ulysses and sat in the corner of the sofa before he answered. 'My life's an open book.'

'It's not you I'm going to ask about.'

Ulysses said, 'Don't ask Dad! I'll tell you about me!'

And Deidre, gay and giggly, 'It's not you either, Ulysses.'

I didn't look at Alexander but I felt something pass between us. It was an urgent plea. For what? I cried out to him. Nothing came back but silence.

I laughed. 'You don't need to look so solemn, Crispin! I only want to know what you meant just now when you said that Alexander and I had something in common.'

Tension whipped round the four of them. I had spoken lightly, maybe thoughtlessly and provocatively, but I hadn't anticipated this sharp united reaction.

Deidre moved from my side. She went to the table where the silver champagne container glistened with ice and condensation and stood beside Alexander. She drew herself to her full height and still her head scarcely reached to his shoulder. Her eyes were huge. Her lower lip trembled.

I was sick with disgust at myself. I searched frantically for something to say. I could find no words to ease the pain I had so unforgiveably inflicted on Deidre.

I tore my gaze from hers and looked at Crispin. He sat relaxed and smiling. It was Ulysses who answered.

'Father was remarking on the fact that of all of us at Hawkridge you and Alexander are the only ones who smoke.'

I looked him full in the eyes. What had been no more than an idle comment from Crispin was disquieting from Ulysses. Why should he want to link Alexander with me? Or me with Alexander? I wouldn't give him the satisfaction of knowing that he had disturbed me.

I said, withering him, 'Neither you nor your father need bother yourselves about it. I don't smoke.' I crushed out the cigarette and grinned at him.

'No . . . No!'

It was after dinner. Well fed and well wined, I walked with Deidre up the side scarlet staircase, sharing girl talk. She had recovered, in fact she had been the life of the dinner party, displaying an amusing and often witty turn of mind. As we walked along the left-hand side of the gallery I was happy and fully relaxed, so that when she opened the door of her bedroom and let out a terrified sound and hid her face in her hands my reaction was slow.

'What is it, Deidre?'

'Can you see it?'

I looked. 'See what?'

'The curtains are open.'

There were two windows, one on each wall of the angle of the room. The glass shone blackly against the night.

'Emma!'

A hand gripped my wrist. 'It's all right, Deidre.'

'I drew them myself.'

I stared at the black holes into the black night. 'Maybe you thought you did.'

'I did! I always do!'

'Maybe one of the servants . . .'

Her body was convulsed with shivers. I felt them in

the hand that tightened on my wrist. 'It was him.'

'Which him?' I said, not yet frightened, still in the happy haze created by Alexander's wines.

'Is it there?'

A chill raced along my spine. 'There's nothing,' I said. 'Except that we've both had our fair share of drink.'

Her head came up. Her eyes were drenched with fear, the pupils huge and black. 'Emma! Can you see it?'

'See what?'

'The light.'

'Oh, is that what you want!' I put out my hand and the room came alive as I pressed the switch.

'No, no, no!' Her voice rose. 'Stop treating me like a child.'

'Then stop behaving like one.'

'I've seen it! I tell you I've seen it.'

'Seen what?' I asked.

'The light from the marshes.'

'You can't see The Chains from here.'

She didn't hear me. 'I've seen it—the blue light.'

Her terror reached out and touched me. 'What blue light?' I snapped.

'Will-o'-the-wisp.'

'You can't see the marsh from here, Deidre,' I repeated.

'It'll get me.' She was whimpering, giving small cries like a dreaming puppy. 'One day it'll dance for me and I'll follow.'

I could believe her as I looked away from her and out into the night. I felt the pull of the high and desolate marshland, the brooding loneliness of the narrow valley and rough steep hills that led up to Pinkery Pond and The Chains. I felt the shadows rising in a pool of darkness, falling down he hills, until at last Hawkridge

Manor was drowned in the black waters.

'No one comes back from that dance.'

I came back with a start. 'Let me go.'

She began to hum the waltz low in her throat.

I said loud and clear, 'Let go!'

Even as I gave my order I knew that she couldn't obey. I put my hand on hers and pried open the fingers. She turned at once, and pressed her body against the lintel of the door. The disquieting frightening little gasps were muffled.

'I'm going to draw the curtains now, Deidre.'

She didn't answer. I walked quickly across the room. The curtain rattled as I pulled the cord of first one and then the other window. The result was magic.

When I turned she was coming into the room, the gaiety on her again as if she slipped it on like a second shining dress.

'I *am* a silly girl!'

'Are you?'

'I can't bear to see windows after nightfall. All the curtains are always drawn at twilight.' The words were pouring out of her. 'It's this house. So isolated. Those horrible dark woods at the back. It'd be easy for someone to hide there and come creeping up to the house. I see this face, you see. I know it's silly, up here on the first floor. I have a vivid imagination and I see it, all white and puffy with staring eyes. A peeping Tom.'

She sat on a pink velvet stool and began to peer at her own face in the mirror.

'A face?' I echoed. 'Just now it was a blue light.'

Her spine stiffened. Then she laughed. 'That's my pseudonym for The Face. Being scared of a blue will-o'-the-wisp is acceptable. Everyone knows they live on the marshlands and lure their victims to a watery grave. But to be frightened by a face isn't acceptable. Alexander gets absolutely furious with me.'

'So you pretend.'

'That's right. I pretend.' She looked at my reflection in the mirror and smiled at me. 'You believe me, don't you, Emma?'

'Believe what?'

'What I tell you.'

'Which should I believe? Peeping Tom? Or the will-o'-the-wisp?'

'It doesn't matter. Just believe me!'

I didn't answer but that didn't seem to matter either.

She picked up a bottle of scent and sprayed it on her neck. The perfume was too sweet for my taste and I turned away to look at her bedroom. It was a feminine room, pink and white with frills and flounces on everything. The head of the four poster bed was like a circus candy floss. Only one side of the spread of white sheet was turned down. On it there was a froth of pink nightdress and a matching bedjacket. No pyjamas.

The wine swirled in my head. I felt dizzy but it wasn't only the wine. I had to get away from Deidre, from her girlish chatter and disturbing changes of mood. I had to be alone, to let my hope free for a moment before I flung caution to the winds. There was a door to the left of the head of the bed.

'I'll be back in a moment,' I said.

'Okay.'

My hand was on the handle when she shouted, 'Not *that* room!'

I jerked round. She was on her feet, her face ashen. 'I'm sorry,' I said. 'Isn't this the bathroom?'

'No, it isn't. *That's* the bathroom.'

She pointed to a door on the far side of the room. I didn't say anything. I walked past her and shut the bathroom door behind me but I couldn't shut her out of my mind.

I looked at myself in the mirror over the basin but I didn't see my reflection. I saw Deidre's fear-drenched eyes.

If she was right, and certainly her terror had been genuine, someone had come into her room and opened her curtains with malice aforethought. 'It was him,' she had said, and in my state of bibulous geniality I hadn't asked which man she accused. One thing was certain. After my arrival all three men had been present, so if it *was* one of the Brett males it must have been done before I arrived.

I saw the hall again. I searched memory for anything that might give me the answer. For, the more I thought, the more I realised that it wasn't only for Deidre that I must learn the truth. I needed to know for myself.

I saw Ulysses beside the front door, Alexander by the door to the drawing room, and Crispin at the foot of the stairs. The torch! In Crispin's hand, still alight! I examined the image of him in my memory and it didn't jell with the image of a man creeping into a girl's bedroom to draw back the curtains in a cruel practical joke.

Ulysses? From his reputation and from my experience with him in the churchyard he was an even more unlikely candidate. When Ulysses played a trick of cruelty it was done in the open. Ulysses enjoyed watching the effect on his victims.

Alexander? No! I rejected the possibility with all the

strength that was in me. I wouldn't even consider it.

My thoughts went back to Deidre. What was it that she had seen? What was it that had appeared to her in the black night beyond the window? As I asked myself that question I realised I was admitting that she had seen *something*.

I knew, too, with a chilling understanding, that by my admission *I* was involved. I was suddenly sober. I would have to uncover the answer—no matter who it destroyed.

CHAPTER NINE

THE LONGEST weekend of my life finally came to an end but Alexander didn't contact me.

I drifted through those days and nights, dreaming about a life at Hawkridge Manor. I didn't know it but these were the last days when my own common sense would be overshadowed by the romantic ideals of my father. I saw myself as the Lady of the Manor, dispensing charm and justice to all around me. I saw myself at Alexander's side and, for it was an essential part of my dream, I obliterated any thoughts of Deidre.

I tried to obliterate Deidre but her face had the habit of popping up between me and the table I was dusting or the crockery I was washing or the road I was driving.

On the Monday, in the hope that I might have a chance encounter with Alexander, I drove to Dunster and to Minehead and went browsing round his shops. I didn't find him.

All I found was an increasing disgust with myself and my behaviour.

On Tuesday I mooched around the cottage. I had done my bit; now it was up to him. I listened for the telephone but it didn't ring. Twice I went and lifted the receiver in the conviction that he was trying to phone and the line was out of order. It wasn't.

I was short-tempered with my aunt to the point of being what my father would have pronounced churlish, and worse, discourteous. The fact that Aunt Victoria never gave me back a harsh word, only looked at me with sympathy, added to my boorish behaviour.

So, at last, sometime during the unending night of the fifth of May, lying in bed and watching the almost-full moon float across my window, I knew what I must do.

I was up early. By the time Aunt Victoria came down at eight the kettle was boiling. She gave me a shrewd glance.

'Morning, Emma.'

'I couldn't sleep.'

She sat at the table where I had laid the grapefruit that was her unvarying breakfast. The toast popped up and I poured the water into the teapot. I sat opposite her. I poured the tea and passed her a cup. I burned my mouth in my unthinking haste to drink the night away. And my Aunt Victoria went quietly on with her grapefruit.

'It's time I went back to London,' I said.

'Yes, Emma.'

'Why don't you say it?'

'Say what?'

'I told you so.'

She gave me a quick smile. 'If it'll help I will.'

I grimaced. 'You warned me.'

'I hoped you'd listen.'

'I got burned. And not just my tongue with the tea.'

'If you rush into things . . .'

'Oh, not badly! Even I can't get badly burned in such a short time.'

'But it's not like that, is it Emma?'

'No.' I caught my breath.

She lifted her shoulders in a small affectionate shrug. 'It's never a question of the length of time. It's the degree of the burn. I know how close you were to your Father and that his death left a vacuum in your life. Nature won't have a vacuum.'

'It isn't only that, Aunt Victoria.'

'Isn't it?'

'It can't be.'

'Alexander's an attractive man. Especially to someone like you.'

'Why me?' I asked but I knew myself and said, before she could answer, 'You don't have to tell me! I'm always wide open to anyone who's unhappy. Daddy used to say I'd only got to see a lame dog to build a stile to help it over!'

'He was the same,' she said.

I looked at her and I knew that the wound had begun to heal. I had naturally, without the spasm in my throat or the pain in my heart, brought my father into the conversation.

Aunt Victoria said, 'You—both of you—make me mad!'

'I apologise,' I laughed. 'On behalf of my parent and myself.'

It was then that Alexander's car stopped outside the gate.

I was on my feet. He got out of the Jenson and, for a moment, I saw him with the clear eyes of a stranger and I liked what I saw. Then he turned towards the cottage, and I fell in love with him all over again.

'He looks lonely,' I said.
'Alexander Brett is a lonely man.'
The gate clicked.
'Tense.'
'His wife has a manic-depressive psychosis.'
He was coming up the path between the daffodils that had burst into golden bloom in the sunshine of the past days.
'I don't have to build a stile!'
'Emma!'
Her voice whipped at my high-flying hope. I looked at her and grimaced again. 'I know,' I said.
'No you don't. Alexander Brett *is* lonely. He has got a difficult problem in his wife. And other problems, so long as his uncle and his cousin live in his house. But don't misunderstand the man. Alexander Brett is no lame dog!"
'You're telling me that he's come here for himself and not for me.'
'Oh, Emma.' She smiled briefly. 'I don't know why he's here. I doubt if *he* knows. It's you I care about. Keep one foot on the ground!'
'I'll try,' I said and ran to answer his knock on the door.

Half an hour later I stood at Alexander's side by the closed door of his wife's bedroom.

He had said nothing on the drive and next to nothing when I had opened the front door to him.

Very polite, very controlled, he had said, 'Deidre isn't well. She's asking for you. I would appreciate it if you would come to her.'

I had answered him in the same polite controlled manner. 'Of course I'll come.'

'I wonder . . .' He hesitated.

'Ask me,' I told him.

'Would you bring some things for the night?'

He looked at me and the memory of sharp-scented logs and leaping flames, of myself in his green shirt and brown Daks, of brown-shelled eggs and coffee and quiet talk, was between us. But down below was a layer of control that would not be broken by either of us. Not now, while Deidre waited.

'Of course,' I told him. 'I won't be a moment.'

As I turned from him I thought I saw in his eyes that he understood the effort it cost me to keep my voice level and then I remembered my Aunt Victoria's words. No lame dog, I told myself. One foot on the ground. But I knew that even with both feet planted flat and firm on common sense the heart has reasons of its own, and a tendency to take wing with a total contempt for any attempt to stay earthbound.

'This way,' he said now, and opened the door.

I followed him in the pink and white room. 'I thought you said Deidre had locked herself in.'

'She has. Not here. In there.'

He stopped a couple of feet from the door by the head of the four poster. For a moment I did a time-slip. The sheets were neatly turned down, the pink chiffon nightdress was neatly laid out.

'She didn't go to bed last night,' he said.

I was back in the present, in the cold light of day.

'Mary said . . .'

I broke in. 'Mary?'

'Deidre's personal maid.'

'Or nurse?'

'Maid. Mary said she found the bed like that when she brought tea this morning.' He gave me a sharp look. 'Deidre doesn't need a nurse.'

'I—I only thought—' I was floundering.

He came to my aid. 'She is in the care of Dr. Hallet. She has these fluctuating moods. You've seen her. But she isn't certifiable.'

'Of course not. I didn't mean it like that.'

'There are people who do mean it. And who say it.'

What can I say to you, Alexander? What words can I find that will be enough and not too much? There are no words. Aware of my failure, I say, 'Aunt Victoria didn't.'

'I like your Aunt Victoria.'

'Me, too.'

He had been looking at the door all this time and now he turned his head and looked at me. His eyes were steady. In the silence I felt that he must hear the wild beat of my heart but if he did he made no response.

One foot on the ground! Alexander Brett is not the man to let emotion run away with him. Even if he feels anything more than friendship for you, this is not the moment.

'Shouldn't you knock?' I asked.

'You're not afraid?'

'Of Deidre?'

'No,' he said. 'You wouldn't be.'

I gave him back the straight look. 'Is there something you haven't told me?'

Did he hesitate? I couldn't be sure.

'The only danger,' he said in the polite controlled voice again, 'is to herself. As she's asking for you she's still aware of the world around her.'

His voice went on but I could scarcely hear him now, the distance was great between us.

I said loud and clear, 'It's time. Tell her I'm here.'

A spasm tightened his mouth. 'Dr. Hallet is coming in after surgery,' he said. 'I'll stay here.'

Suddenly I knew what I must do. 'No, Alexander.'

'You may need me.'

'But Deidre won't.'

He looked at me in another long moment of silence. And then he turned from me and walked away from me. I watched him. He didn't look back. He was gone.

I heard the faint click of a turning key and I spun to face the inner door. Deidre must have been just inside, listening, her ear pressed against the wood.

I waited. I waited for the door to open, my heart hammering, my mouth dry. Not out of fear for myself but because I was in a panic that I would fail her.

The door remained shut.

I sent out a prayer that I would know what to do. I took a deep breath. I put out my hand. The china knob was cold. I opened the door and looked into a nursery.

Like the bedroom the decor was pink and white. The room was fully furnished, but there was no fire in the grate and the air was musty as if the windows were never opened There was wall-to-wall pink carpeting but there was no speck of dirt, no untidied toy on the smooth surface.

This was an empty room, an abandoned room. No child played or laughed or cried in this immaculate nursery. Yet in the old-fashioned child-size hip bath on the floor there was a family of pink ducks floating on two inches of water. White towels hung on the rail behind the bath.

A door of the pink wardrobe was open and I saw a row of turn of the century babies' dresses with tiny flaring sleeves and bodices of handmade lace and long skirts of voile.

In the angle of the room there was a baby's cot in wicker-work and mahogany, suspended on carved posts, one at each end. Beneath the curved wicker-work hood I saw a pink-faced baby doll. Propped up on a white lace pillow, tiny pink arms stretching up to me, the long white dress spreading down to the foot of the cot, it stared back at me, unwinking. The cot was swinging gently to and fro as if it had recently been set in motion.

I looked at Deidre and the marrow froze in my bones. I forgot Alexander. I knew that only if I used every last ounce of common sense and love could I get Deidre back from the place where she had gone.

Deidre sat on a chair beside the empty grate. Her long hair was a spun gold shawl around her shoulders hiding her face. She rocked back and forth, singing. It wasn't a song for a little girl. She sang, low and crooning, so tender that my heart ached, 'The Grand Old Duke of York.'

There was a chair strategically placed at the opposite side of the empty grate. I walked to it. As I sat down I saw that she cuddled a second doll on her lap. Hidden by her long hair I could only see brown sandals and jean-covered legs.

It was enough.

I asked, casually, 'How's Jason this morning?'

She rocked to and fro. The singing stopped.

'Deidre,' I said, 'you want to talk to me?' Silence.

The rocking stopped. She was motionless behind the veil of her hair. 'You told Alexander to . . .'

'I don't want to see him.'

I leaned towards her. At least I was in contact with her. 'You don't have to see him,' I assured her.

'He tried to take Jason away from me.'

'When?'

'This morning. Very early.'

'Where?'

'I said Alexander *tried* to take Jason away from me.'

'I'm sorry.'

'That's all right.'

'Where would he try to take Jason?'

'To my mother, of course.'

'Of course,' I agreed.

'But he hasn't.'

We were going in circles. I had to break out.

'Deidre,' I said, firm and clear, 'why do you say that Alexander hasn't taken Jason away from you?'

She shivered. A small burst of song came from her and I wanted to kick myself for my blunder.

I could only try again. 'Deidre, I do want to help you.'

'Are you blind?'

I took a deep breath. 'It's difficult to see beneath all your hair.'

'I'm telling you.'

'Telling me what?'

'He hasn't got him.'

'*You've* got Jason!' Deliberately, I taunted her.

'Really, Emma, if you're going to be stupid you'd better go.'

I accepted her challenge. 'If that is what you want,' I said, half standing.

My trick worked. 'Sit down,' she said. 'Look.' She opened her arms but kept her head bent. 'Now can you see I've got Jason?'

I looked. The doll wore an emerald green jersey, its close-cropped curls were dark against her breast. Its eyes stared back at me, as blank as the eyes of the baby doll in the cot. For the first time I realised that Deidre was fully clothed. It shook my heart to see that she had dressed the doll to match her own jeans and jersey.

'Yes,' I said. 'I can see you've got Jason.'

'He won't take Jason from me.'

'Why would he want to take your son away from you?'

At last I reached into the dark corner of the mind. Her head came up. Her face beneath the veil of her hair was like marble, blank with grief and bewilderment.

'Alexander took my baby from me.'

I stared at her, caught in my own confusion.

'Tell me about it,' I said.

She shivered again. Her arms tightened on the Jason doll.

'Ulysses said *I* did it.'

I looked at her in sudden helplessness. I hadn't reached her. I had only stirred up the swirling mud of a deeper suffering.

'She was so beautiful. Like a doll. So tiny. Her hands were flowers. She was so quiet. She just lay in her cot and slept. When she was awake she was quiet. Just lay and looked up at me with huge blue eyes. Empty eyes. I wanted her to cry. I shook her. I held her naked little body after her bath. She smelled so sweet. And I shook her. But she didn't cry.'

She stopped. There was nothing I could do but listen. I said, 'What happened to your baby, Deidre?'

'Ulysses said *I* did it.' She stared at me through the tears that welled into her eyes.

'What did Ulysses say you did to your baby?' I repeated quietly.

'He said I got angry. He said I threw her into her cot. He said I put a pillow over her head.'

I looked at her and I couldn't believe that it had been as Ulysses said. And why Ulysses? I put the question away for the moment.

'Deidre,' I asked, keeping my voice quiet and firm. 'Is that what happened?'

'I can't remember!' she shouted.

Something in her eyes didn't match the hysterical shout. 'Are you sure you can't?' I asked.

'I want to. When I think about it my head begins to hurt inside, in the middle of my brain.' A single tear fell down her cheek. 'Oh, Emma! Help me! I *must* remember!'

I shifted on the chair, ashamed of my momentary doubts. 'I'll try and help,' I said.

'I didn't kill my baby.' Her eyes clung to mine in a plea of desperation. 'You believe me, don't you Emma?'

I couldn't sustain her look. I lowered my eyes and inspected my own hands as they twisted round each other.

'Why should you? No one else does.'

I made myself look up at her again. 'Try me,' I said.

She drew a long shuddering breath. She pressed her white face to the face of the Jason doll and the words came fast in a low monotone. 'I came in here that morning. I looked after my babies myself. After her two a.m. feed I had put Dawn on her right side.'

I broke in. 'How old was she?'

'Seven months and seven days. She couldn't take much food at one time so Dr. Hallet said to keep on feeding her little and often. It was just getting light when I came to her again. A blackbird was singing. I looked in the cot. She was lying on her face.'

'She had turned over in he night,' I said, and drew a breath of relief. This was a tragedy but not a crime.

'Dawn couldn't turn herself. Dr. Hallet said that some babies take a long time.'

'I'm sure they do,' I said.

'I looked at my baby,' Deidre began to shiver again, 'lying on her face. I picked her up. She was cold. I wrapped her in a shawl and held her inside my dressing gown.' The shivering became shudders that shook her from head to foot. 'Her little body was cold.'

'Deidre,' I said but she didn't hear me.

'Alexander, I called. Come and help me. I'd left him in bed. He was still asleep. I couldn't move. I screamed at him.' She stopped and her arms fell away from the boy doll. It sat bolt upright, precariously balanced on her lap.

'It was Alexander,' she said, 'Alexander,' she repeated, 'killed my baby!'

I stared at her twisted face. This accusation was what my Aunt Victoria had told me but I couldn't believe it. Deidre's mind had been unhinged by her loss.

'That's a terrible thing to say.' She didn't hear me but I had to go on. 'Didn't the doctor tell you . . .'

She broke in, cold and frightened. 'I loved my baby.'

'And Alexander?' This touched her. I leaned towards her and tried to hold the contact. 'Dawn was his daughter, too.'

I had said the wrong thing. She went back into herself,

back into the dark world. 'It was Alexander,' she repeated tonelessly.

I couldn't help her. I could only try and sort out my own peace of mind. 'And you told people that it was Alexander?'

'Of course.'

'Of course,' I echoed.

'It's the truth.'

'Is it?' She didn't answer. Her eyes were as blank as those of the doll children. 'Deidre, you've got to accept the fact of what happened to your baby.'

'Alexander took my baby away from me.'

I could see them—the distraught mother clinging to her child; Alexander, shocked into action—and my heart ached for both of them.

'Alexander,' she said, 'forced my arms open and he took her away. This morning he took Jason.'

She shivered violently. The doll slipped on her knees. I put out my hand but I was too late. Deidre's arms snatched at him wildly, and it was as if she lashed out at him. The Jason doll fell off her lap. It broke its head on the edge of the metal fireguard.

I looked up at her in horror. I braced my body, ready for violence. I tightened my mind, ready for hysterics.

I found neither. It was as if the breaking of the doll had had a cathartic effect. Colour came back to her cheeks, the mist cleared out of her eyes, she smiled at me and, when she spoke, her voice was warm and friendly.

'Sometimes,' she said, ignoring the doll with its shattered head lying at her feet, 'I'm a little scared of my husband.'

'Of Alexander?' I stared at Deidre, stunned by the change in her.

'He's so dominating!' She leaned her elbows on her knees and cradled her face in her hands. 'Every woman wants to be dominated. I know that. But sometimes Alexander goes overboard. He can be absolutely ruthless.'

'Maybe,' I said drily, 'he has to make decisions.'

'Of course he does. I'm not running him down.' Her eyelids narrowed. The tears were gone and she was very gay. 'He doesn't love me.'

I stared at her. My mouth went dry and I couldn't speak.

Deidre laughed. 'Don't look so shocked. He never loved me. I knew that when I married him.'

I swallowed. 'Then why did he marry you?'

'Pity.'

'You knew this, too?'

'Yes.'

'And you still married him?'

'Yes.'

There was something I was missing, something of supreme importance. It was there, on the edge of my mind, like a tune that slips down into the subconscious when one tries to grab at a line of melody.

Deidre said, and I put aside what I couldn't remember, 'It's so simple, Emma. Alexander's strong.' She spoke in a bright gay voice. 'I've always been dominated by him. When we were kids together, the three of us, we'd play father and mother. It was always Alexander and me. We made Ulysses our child.' Her laugh was mocking. 'Ulysses didn't like it. But he learned that he hadn't any choice. If he wanted to play with Alexander and me he had to do what we wanted.'

'But Ulysses was the eldest.'

'He was.' She laughed again and there was the cruelty of children in her. 'But Alexander and I, together, were stronger. Invincible!'

'I bet you were.'

'There was a terrific sibling rivalry between the two boys.'

'And you,' I said slowly, 'enjoyed fanning the flames?'

'It was fun!' Her eyes flashed. 'Exciting.'

I stood up. 'Dangerous,' I said, 'if you still enjoy it.'

She got up and put a hand on my arm and melted into the innocent pleading. 'Oh, Emma! I know . . . I hate myself for it but I can't stop!'

I felt myself responding. 'Oh . . . Deidre,' I said helplessly.

I looked at her and I wondered just how much of her manic-depressive psychosis was genuine, and how much of it was the deliberate effort to remain in the exciting love-savage world of her childhood importance between Alexander and Ulysses.

She gave me no time to think. Her hands tightened.

'You're the only person I can trust,' she said. 'No, don't laugh at me. I've only got a little time. Tomorrow is the night of the full moon. I know he's going to do something.'

'Alexander?'

She stared at me. 'Stay with me! I'm frightened!

'Who do you mean by *he*?'

She shook her head and her hair flew around her in a shining stream. She let go of my arm and buried her face in her hands. 'That's it!' she whispered. 'I don't know. They want me out. All those Brett men want me out.'

I stared back at her. 'Crispin?' I mocked.

'You think he's a harmless old gentleman!' Her head flung back and her gaze hit my eyes.

'Well . . .'

She gave me no time to even consider what I felt about Crispin. 'He's as harmless as a rattlesnake. The perfect charmer until you get in his way. Then watch out! He's not even that old! Certainly not old enough to have spent all passion.'

'Are you telling me that Crispin wants an affair with you?'

'Crispin! Me!'

'No,' I said drily.

'Crispin wants Hawkridge Manor. He's wanted it since he came into the world six minutes after Christian. All his life he's been riddled with envy, full of bitterness. He hates everyone. Except Ulysses.'

I shook my head. 'It doesn't make sense, Deidre. Why should he want to be rid of you?'

'It's really very simple.'

'It is?'

'Yes. Crispin wants Hawkridge Manor for his son. I ruined any chance of that happening when I married Alexander and gave Jason to him.'

'*Gave* Jason?'

She ignored this. I felt as if she was playing her own game, using me in some way that I couldn't understand. Or was it simply that her mind had been thrown out of balance by the death of her baby daughter?

She said, as if she caught my thought. 'I'm not mad, Emma.'

'Then you're deliberately trying to stir things up?'

'It's not only me. They're in it. Both of them. Oh, Emma . . .'

Her eyes stretched wide again and she was none of the things I had thought about her. She was a frightened girl in a house of suppressed and violent emotions.

I said, 'Just for the record, Ulysses wants . . .'

She broke in. 'Ulysses wants anything that Alexander has.'

'And Alexander? What does Alexander want in all this?'

'Alexander wants . . .'

CHAPTER TEN

I didn't hear what she said for it was lost in a sudden crescendo of shouting. My gaze flew to the door. My heart jerked.

'You stay here, Deidre.'

'They're coming.'

'I'll get rid of them.'

The voices were loud now, angry. I couldn't hear more than a few disjointed words for they shouted each other down.

'Oh, no,' Deidre said. 'I won't miss this! But not in here. I won't have them in the nursery. Quick, Emma! Into the bedroom.'

I stared at her. She was quivering with excitement. Her eyes were brilliant. Her lower lip was caught between her teeth. There was a wildness in her that set my own nerves leaping.

'Deidre!' I cried. 'Stop it!'

Her answer was a shove in the small of my back. I shot into the bedroom in front of her. She was beside me. The door to the nursery closed as Ulysses burst in through the other door with Alexander close on his heels.

'Gentlemen!'

Both men froze at the sound of her contempt. Alexander stood six feet tall and straight but Ulysses' huge body seemed to dwarf him. Alexander was a white-hot fury. Ulysses was disarmingly controlled. Ulysses looked at Deidre with a smouldering anticipation. Alexander's eyes were black ice, dangerous.

Tension held the three of them. They had faced each other like this many times, but I sensed that this time was different. The power that the three of them had generated over the years was now explosive, unstable.

I said, 'Hallo, Alexander.' He nodded but didn't look at me. 'Morning, Ulysses,' I said but didn't get even a nod.

Deidre, her voice full of laughter, said, 'It's a long time since I had the pleasure of the Brett cousins coming running to see me!' She turned to me, eyes wide with innocence. 'Now, Emma, you can see for yourself.' She turned back to look at the men. 'Aren't they just magnificently moody!'

I looked at them. Ulysses grinned at her. Alexander's gaze flicked my eyes and I felt the burning ice before he looked back at his wife.

'Well, boys,' Deidre said. 'What can I do for you?'

Ulysses took a step forward. Alexander didn't move. My throat contracted in a nervous giggle. I opened my mouth, but before I could speak Ulysses shouted, 'Where's Jason?'

'Ask Alexander,' Deidre shouted back at him.

'Don't shout,' Alexander shouted.

I laughed. It was a nervous reaction, an irruption of

tension that had nothing at all to do with humour. It worked. For a moment.

Alexander said, 'Let's all go downstairs and have coffee.'

'Good idea,' I said, my enthusiasm bubbling from me, forced and false. 'How about it, Deidre?'

She was watching Ulysses as if, when Alexander turned to me, she let go of him to concentrate on the other man.

'Well, Ulysses?' she asked. 'Are you ready for drawing room coffee?'

My fists clenched. I could happily have given her a hearty slap. What did she want? Didn't she understand that provocation resulted in reaction? But of course she did! This was her entertainment.

'No,' Ulysses said, smiling a huge white-toothed smile, 'I'm not. Are you?'

'Not if you're not.'

Ulysses came slowly across the room. His hand trailed round the posts at the foot of the bed and fell to his side again. I heard Deidre's quick intake of breath and shot a look at Alexander.

He hadn't moved. He stood just inside the open door, a fine tension in every line of his body. His gaze was unfalteringly fixed on Deidre. I tried to read what lay behind his eyes but he was hidden behind the mask of his watchful concentration. I wanted desperately to see in his eyes if his fury was promoted by love. I could see nothing. I could feel nothing coming from him. He wasn't it seemed, aware of my presence.

Ulysses asked again, only a fraction less violent, 'Where's Jason?'

'Gone,' she said in her light little girl voice.

I went cold. This was their moment. This was what the

three of them had been moving towards through the years of their sibling jealousies and rivalries.

I wanted to get away. I didn't want to see or hear any more of their mutual torture. I didn't want to see Alexander so involved. "I'll go get that coffee.'

Deidre cried, 'Please, Emma! You promised!'

Smiling at me, Ulysses said, 'Don't miss the next exciting instalment.'

Alexander didn't look at me. 'Emma,' he said, 'You'd better stay.'

Did I hear an appeal beneath the flat voice? Or did I hear it because I wanted to? 'All right,' I said, light as a breath. 'Since you all want me, I'll stay.'

Ulysses took another step forward so that he was within reaching distance. I wished that Alexander would move up to join us but he stood still.

'I'll ask you once more, Deidre.'

'And then what?' Her head flung back in defiance.

He asked again, each word separated, bounding at her like a slate over water. 'Where is Jason?'

'Gone.'

'Gone where?'

'Away from you.'

The blood suffused his face. The easy good humour fell from him like a discarded coat. He was angry, ugly in face and mood.

'I told you Jason was not to go to that woman again.'

Her lip curled. 'Do you really think I'd hide him away from you there!'

'So!' The blood poured out of his face. There were small grey patches at the corners of his nostrils. His hair was a blaze of red against the white skin. 'You admit it!'

'I admit nothing!'

'The truth, Deidre.'

'You know the truth, Ulysses.'

Her eyes flashed. There was a wild and dangerous excitement in her as she stared up into his face.

'*I* know it,' Ulysses said.

'Then you can mind your own business.'

'Jason is my business.'

'Oh, sure, *Uncle* Ulysses!'

I thought he would strike her then but he controlled himself with a visible effort. 'It's time, Deidre,' he said, quiet and low, in a whisper that reached to the edges of the room. 'Tell us. All of us. Now, Deidre. The truth.'

Her disintegration was painful. As he spoke the fire went out of her. Her body shrank, her eyes emptied. She looked fragile and delicate. It was impossible that she could ever have been the malicious and provocative child I had witnessed only a moment ago.

'I don't know what you mean,' she whimpered.

'Oh, but you do.'

'Alexander . . .'

Ulysses moved so that he was between her and his cousin. He towered over her. There was no shadow but it seemed as if she was within the shadow of his body.

'Alexander can't help you now, Deidre.'

'I'm his wife.'

'You cheated me.'

There was a brief flash of spirit. 'And what did you do to me?'

'I loved you.'

'Love! You wanted me.'

'Of course I wanted you.'

'Not me! You never even saw *me*!'

I glanced from Deidre to Ulysses and wished I hadn't. I looked quickly away, across to Alexander but he was enclosed in the wall of silence.

'Of course I saw you,' Ulysses said impatiently. 'Don't start that sick talk again.'

'*You're* sick! Leave me alone!'

'I will,' he said. 'When you tell Alexander the truth.'

'You see! You're still at it! Anything, no matter how it hurts or who it hurts, to spite Alexander.'

'Tell him!'

'All right! I'll tell you the truth! You seduced me. You made what you call love to me. Love! You didn't know the first thing about loving. I hate you for what you did to me.'

Ulysses said, 'Go on.'

And now, at last, Alexander came to stand by the dressing table. 'If you can,' he said as gently as if he spoke to a frightened child.

Deidre took in a sharp audible breath. The three of us waited. I thought that she was extracting the last ounce of drama by making us wait but when I looked at her I saw that she was unable to speak. Her lips moved and her throat contracted but no sound came out.

'For God's sake!' I cried. 'Stop this!'

My outburst was the flashpoint.

I took a step towards Deidre. It was my intention to get her out of the room.

One minute I was going forward under my own volition. The next, Ulysses' hand was flat on my chest, his forefinger and thumb squeezing my windpipe so that I snatched at a breath. And then I was skidding backwards.

It was Deidre who caught me. Her arms came round

me, I smelled the sweet fragrance of her perfume and the room took the right position again.

I had never seen men fight. I always believed that physical violence would fill me with revulsion. When Alexander made his move the adrenalin flowed in my blood, flames of excitement flicked and spat along my nerve ends and I felt a great shout welling up from a part of me that I had never known before.

The fever only lasted a moment.

At my side I heard Deidre's sharp intake of breath. I shot a look at her and was sickened by the sight of my own sensations made visible on her face.

I turned back. I saw the cold hard anger in Alexander. I saw the mocking grin on Ulysses as he watched me. I saw Alexander's hand come up and I was sick with fear for him.

Alexander caught Ulysses by the arm that had sent me stumbling. He swung him round and got in one quick jab on Ulysses' left eye. Then Ulysses recovered from the shock of surprise and the fight became a matter of Ulysses' thudding fists and Alexander's helpless effort to get through the whirlwind.

'Ulysses!'

Crispin came into the doorway. From the lips of this quiet courteous man there came a commando's shout.

I had time to see Crispin, to see the dark suited stranger at his side and then I looked back at Alexander.

For a split second Ulysses looked at his father. In that instant Alexander hit his chin. He was falling. But even as he fell the great fist came up in a retaliatory blow and Alexander reeled.

Ulysses fell, grabbing wildly at the bed. His fingers, tearing for a hold, caught the pink nightdress and carried it to the floor. He rolled over onto his back and stayed there. The nightdress draped around him and he lay on the floor, laughing.

Alexander, tripping over the seat, hit the back of his head on the corner of the dressing table, and went down with blood already falling onto the white fur rug.

I wanted to go to him but Deidre's fingers gripped my arm. Before I could release myself the stranger was kneeling at his side. Lifting him to a sitting position, he said, 'A handkerchief;' and pressed his hand against the wound as the blood ran down Alexander's neck.

I looked round wildly.

'Quickly!'

I dragged my arm from Deidre's grip and was in and out of the nursery.

'Here!' I held out the child's towels from the rail by the bath.

The stranger said, 'Make one into a pad.'

I folded it. 'Like this?'

'Fine.'

The stranger took it and pressed it on the back of Alexander's head. Alexander's blood was red on the man's hand, red on the rug.

'I'm all right,' Alexander said, struggling to get up.

'Stay still! You're bleeding like a stuck pig. Head wounds do that. It'll stop in a minute if you do as you're told. You're lucky that surgery finished early this morning. Very lucky. Isn't that so, Deidre?'

Deidre stared at Alexander.

'I'm all right,' he said gently, speaking directly to her.

Her lip trembled. She was weeping quietly. She gazed long and silently into his eyes. If ever I saw a soul in torment it was Deidre before she turned and went back into the nursery.

'Deidre!' he called.

The door of the nursery shut.

'Be still, Alexander!'

He was on his feet. He held the bloodstained towel to his head and went to the door. 'Deidre . . .'

In the silence the sound of the key was loud.

CHAPTER ELEVEN

Dr. Hallet was grave.

It was after his evening surgery that he came back to Hawkridge Manor.

Alexander, patched up with sticking plaster, had tried to make contact with Deidre. I had tried. Her maid, Mary, had gone alone to the door with a tray at lunchtime and again at teatime.

The door remained closed.

There was no sound from inside the room.

Deidre had gone to ground and this time she rejected all contact.

We were talking in the white drawing room.

Ulysses, the angry bruises that blotched his skin an ugly contrast with the red of his hair, had helped the hours along with a liberal intake of whisky. He wasn't drunk but his smile and his words were inclined to slop around.

Crispin sat upright in a chair beside the fire. Of the three Brett men he was the least outwardly disturbed. Ulysses was tousle-haired. His purple silk shirt was open at the neck, revealing wiry red hair, and his levis were muddy around the hems. Alexander had brushed his hair but he still wore the charcoal slacks and jersey into which he had changed when he removed the bloodstained shirt early that morning.

Only Crispin was immaculately groomed. I couldn't know about his dedicated veneration for a style of living that was finished while he was still a child. I didn't understand that by appearing at eight o'clock in the evening in a lounge suit instead of the formality of a dinner jacket, Crispin Brett betrayed the extent of his disturbance and the depth of his involvement.

Alexander—but I could do no more than glance at him. I couldn't try to get behind the barrier of ashen face and eyes as dark and impenetrable as water on a moonless night. Alexander went through that long day in a pain of his own that commanded respect. I could only wait and be there if he should need me.

Dr. Hallet said, 'I think the time has come to take steps.'

'What do you suggest?'

'Deidre has been increasingly confused in the past weeks.'

Alexander nodded.

Dr. Hallet's voice was an impersonal concern as he quietly probed the wound. 'She's become increasingly distressed.'

'Each time,' Alexander said, the words bitten between tight lips, 'she has swung a little further. The gaiety has grown brighter. The depressions deeper.'

'And Jason?'

Out of the corner of my eye, I saw Crispin stiffen but it was Ulysses who answered.

He had been standing beside the red amber elephant

and now he picked it up and carried it and put it down the table that stood behind the sofa.

'Jason,' he said, his tongue a little thick. 'I gave him the elephant. Christening present. Not a lucky elephant. See. It's got its trunk down.'

He stroked the red amber trunk. His fingers were white. The backs of the digits were thick with red hair. He lifted heavy eyelids and stabbed a forefinger in Doctor Hallet's chest. 'Ask *me* about Jason.'

'I don't see . . .'

'You don't see,' Ulysses mocked.

Alexander said, 'This is not the time, Ulysses.'

Ulysses swung unsteadily on his feet. 'It's never the time! Not for you! Well, now is the time for me.'

Doctor Hallet said, 'Now it's Deidre we . . .'

Ulysses lurched round to face him. He said, loud and clear, 'Jason is *my* son.'

There was silence all around me, a palpable silence that filled the room. The whole house was drowning in silence.

Ulysses' voice came to me from a far distance.

'You were Deidre's doctor. You must know that Jason is my son.'

'I know,' Doctor Hallet told him, 'that you've had your fair share of drink, Ulysses. I suggest you go and sleep it off.'

'Of course!' Ulysses' smile swam all over his face. 'I understand. Professional etiquette.'

'Professional etiquette,' Alexander said, cold and dangerous. 'If you know, Bob—if Deidre told you anything—for God's sake, you must tell me.'

'I'm sorry, Alexander.'

'Sorry? For what? Because you won't speak out?

Because you think I can't take the truth? Because you're protecting my wife?'

'None of these things,' Doctor Hallet said. 'I'm sorry that I can't answer you. Nor Ulysses. I don't know the answer. Deidre never told me anything except the obvious fact that she was three months pregnant.' He paused and added, looking from Alexander to Ulysses and back to Alexander. 'And that she was going to marry you.'

'Damn you!' The blood suffused Ulysses' face. 'You're lying!' He lurched a step closer and thrust his face at the doctor's. 'She told you. She must've told you.'

The doctor's nose curled but he stood his ground. 'No, Ulysses.'

'Jason's my son.'

'Only Deidre knows the truth.'

A sly grin lifted his lips. 'But she didn't say he *wasn't* my son!'

'She didn't discuss the father of her child.'

'Of course she didn't!' Ulysses plunged across the room to stand in front of Alexander. 'All those times when we were kids . . . and you made me look a fool in your games. I've made you the fool now! Let's pretend! Alexander's the father. It was a game then! Now it's no game! Alexander is *not* the father. How does it feel to know you've been made to look a fool, Alexander?'

Alexander said, 'Have you finished?'

'No.'

'I think you have.'

'I want my son.'

'I'm not going to fight you again, Ulysses.'

The blood was thick and hot in Ulysses' face. 'Where is he, Alexander?'

'Safe.'

'I'll find him.'

'I warn you, Ulysses.'

'You warn me!' Ulysses taunted.

'If you try ... If you do anything to Jason, I'll get you.'

I heard my own gasp of indrawn breath. There was no passion in Alexander. He made a cold statement of intention and I was afraid for him. I waited for Ulysses' answering outburst but none came. In a moment Alexander turned and walked to the table. He picked up the red amber elephant and carried it back to its place beneath the window.

Crispin said, 'Doctor Hallet's right, Ulysses. Go and sleep off the drink.'

To my surprise he agreed. 'I'll go. But it's not finished.'

Doctor Hallet said, 'Mr. Brett, perhaps you'll go with him.'

'Of course.' Crispin got to his feet. 'Come, Ulysses.'

Ulysses lurched across the room and went out into the hall without a word.

Crispin paused in the doorway. He stood there a moment, quiet and at ease, but something escaped his control. An electric spark snapped in his eyes as he said, 'I'll be in my room. I'm concerned about Deidre. You'll let me know, Alexander, what you decide to do for her.'

Alexander faced the room.

'Of course I will, Uncle Crispin.'

'Thank you.' He gave a small bow of the head to Alexander and to Doctor Hallet, but not to me. 'I won't go to bed until I hear from you.'

He turned smoothly and shut the door behind him.

I felt a release so strong that I thought I would faint.

There had been an evil spirit in the room. Now that it was gone I was drained. I tried to think, to remember, to find in their words what I must know. Was it Ulysses? Or was it Crispin? Which body did the power of darkness inhabit?

My own mind was confused. All I knew was that I didn't understand, and that all my compassion for Deidre and all my love for Alexander could not lead me to the answer.

But what of the other answer?

Was Jason Alexander's son?

Or was he Ulysses' son?

'Are you all right, Emma?'

My mind cleared. Alexander stood in front of me, his eyes warm with concern.

'I feel a little faint,' I said. 'Silly . . . It'll go in a minute.'

'Come here. I'll open a window.'

Hawkridge Manor had great sash windows. Effortlessly, Alexander pushed the lower half to its highest position. The air came to me from the valley, grass-sweet, evening-cool.

'Thanks,' I said.

He looked into my eyes. 'Stay there,' he said.

I smiled briefly. 'I'm not going anywhere,' I said.

He went back across the room. I heard their voices.

Doctor Hallet talked of forcible entry and, if necessary, forcible removal. He didn't like the idea any more than Alexander liked it. It could be distressing, even harmful, to Deidre. There would be an ambulance, attendants, policemen . . . oh, yes, there had to be police on a certified admission . . . but the nursing home he had in mind was excellent. She would be cared for with all that the medical profession could offer in the way of drugs and compassionate understanding.

I looked out the window. There was an oak tree, quite close to the house, to my left. I hadn't seen it before. But then, I couldn't see it from Deidre's bedroom and when I had dined here (was it really only a five-days-lifetime ago?) the curtains had been drawn. The oak tree was breaking into leaves, pale gold in the evening light.

I looked beyond, all the way up the long green valley with its steep-sided falls of grass. The right-hand slopes were deep purple shadows, but the other side was still awash with the flowing saffron light. Far away, high against the sky, I saw the straight black line that marked the dam of Pinkery Pond.

Alexander was saying, 'You can't mean to take her tonight, Bob.'

'You say she hasn't eaten all day.'

'No. But . . .'

'You took Jason away from her this morning.'

"I had to! These last few days she . . .'

'Battered him?'

I froze. If I had wanted to I couldn't have moved.

'Good God, no! No, Bob! Nothing like that!'

'What then?'

'The opposite. She's ignored him. I found him in the garden yesterday evening. He was crying. Dirty. It was seven o'clock. He was cold and hungry. When I took him to her she was lying on her bed. She looked at us but I'm not sure if she knew us. She took him onto the bed and cuddled him in her arms. She held his head to her breast as if . . .'

He stopped again. Doctor Hallet said, 'As if she thought he was her baby.'

'I thought that she'd got over the death of Dawn.'

Something in his voice released me from my paralysis. He was sitting beside the fire. There was no colour in his face, nor in his lips. His eyes were black glass.

'Go on, Alexander.'

'Oh, God! It's my fault, Bob!'

'Deidre's been disturbed before this.'

'But this time I pushed her over the edge. I forgot. I don't know how I could have forgotten. But I did. It was the first anniversary of Dawn's death. She went to the grave alone.'

He leaned forward and buried his face in his hands. I was across the room before I knew that I had moved. And then, before I reached him, I stopped. His grief was not for me to share.

I turned from him, my arms pressed tight to contain the pain of my helplessness within myself. Doctor Hallet's eyes waited for me, cool and grey. His mind steadied me so that I was able to walk to the sofa and sit on the opposite end from where he sat.

'Doctor Hallet,' I said.

'Yes?'

'May I make a suggestion?'

'Of course.'

'I'm here because Deidre asked for me.' I was aware of Alexander's head lifting but I kept my eyes on the doctor's. 'I had a long talk with her this morning. She trusts me.' I shrugged. 'Maybe because I've got no part in all that's been going on around her.'

'The reason for her trust is unimportant,' Doctor Hallet said. I felt the speculation within him. 'You think you can get through to her?'

'I don't know. I tried. It didn't work.'

'So why should it work next time?'

'When I haven't been in her bedroom, Mary has. It hasn't been left empty. And Deidre hasn't come out of the nursery.' My smile was almost nonexistent. 'I'm enough of a woman to know she won't go through the night without wanting to clean her face and her teeth. Unless, of course, she has gone . . .' I licked my lip with my tongue.

Doctor Hallet helped me. 'The old taboos die hard,' he said gently.

'Let me put it into words for you. Deidre will only remain in her room if her mind has passed from confusion and fear into autism. If, bluntly, she had gone mad.'

'Do you think she has?'

'I don't know. I can only just begin to know her state of mind when I can talk to her.'

'Then let me try to make contact.'

He gave me a shrewd and calculating look. 'What you suggest is that you pass the night in Deidre's bedroom waiting for the moment when she has to go to the bathroom.'

'Yes,' I said. 'If you will tell me what to do and say when she does.'

Alexander said, 'I'll stay with you.'

'No,' I said.

'No, Alexander,' said Doctor Hallet. 'You must keep well away. All of us must keep well away.'

'It's asking too much of Emma.'

'Don't be silly! Deidre's not dangerous!' Doctor Hallet

kept his grey-sea eyes on mine. 'All you can do for her is get her to eat. To drink is even more important. To talk, if you can. The essential thing is to get in communication with her.'

Alexander asked, very quiet now, 'And if she doesn't come out?'

'Then we shall have no choice. Then we will have to take her to the nursing home in the morning.'

'She will have to be certified insane,' he said, even quieter.

'As being a danger to herself.'

Alexander said, 'Emma . . .'

I turned my head and looked at him. 'Don't say anything,' I said. 'Not now.'

There was nothing to say.

A weariness possessed me. I should be hungry. There had been a snack lunch of soup and bread and cheese but only Crispin had eaten. I wasn't hungry.

I lay back in a chair in Deidre's bedroom and watched the light drain out of the sky. The purple shadows, deepening to pansy-black, filled the valley and rose slowly on the tide of night. Soon they flowed down the last slope of the nearest hill. For a little while longer the sheep held the daylight in their fleece, standing on the hill like a child's white cutout farmyard animals, and then they too dissolved slowly into the darkening shadows.

Hawkridge Manor drowned in night.

I lay in the chair, sunk in a lethargy of waiting. The house was quietly waiting all around me. Were they all in their rooms? Did they read? Or walk about? Sleep?

Was Ulysses, or Crispin, or both, sitting, waiting for

the moment when action must be taken? Or Alexander?

And why, in all my own confusion of uncertain loving was I so inexorably certain that one of them must take action. Tonight.

I didn't draw the curtains. I lay looking into the black velvet curtain that night had drawn for me.

Suddenly, light came into the room. I jerked to my feet, my heart thudding, my nerves shooting little catherine wheels of fiery panic all over my body.

I had left the door open onto the landing and I saw that the light came from outside the room. I waited for someone to come into the doorway. Somewhere, at the back of my fear-concentrated mind, I heard the sound of a car going away down the road and made a note that Doctor Hallet was leaving. And then a dark figure was in the doorway, a faceless shape against the background of light and I forgot the car.

'Yes?' I asked.

My voice gave me away.

'It's only me, Miss.' Her arm went up. 'Mary.'

'Don't switch the light on!' I snapped in my relief.

'You can't sit in the dark, Miss.'

'I'm not in the dark with the light from the landing.'

'Very good, Miss.'

I could hear her anxiety. 'I'm waiting in case Mrs. Alexander comes out of her room.' I said quietly. 'There's no bright light. I don't want to do that.'

'No, Miss,' Mary said. She came into the room. 'Mr. Alexander sent you this cup of cocoa.'

'Thank you.' As she moved light glinted on the small silver tray in her hand. 'Put it here, please, Mary.'

She put the tray on the edge of the dressing table and stood, hesitating. 'There's a note, Miss.'

'I see it.' A small white envelope that stilled my heart and quickened my pulse. 'Has . . .' Don't be specific! 'Has everyone gone to bed?'

'I believe so, Miss. There's a bell by Mrs. Alexander's bed. It rings in my room if you need me.'

'Thank you, Mary. I'll do that.'

Still, she hesitated. I caught the gleam of tears in her eyes as she whispered, 'Oh, Miss! It's so sad!'

'Yes.' I agreed.

'Mrs. Alexander's a lovely . . .' She choked. 'I'm sorry, Miss,' she sobbed.

Before I could say anything she darted past me and shot through the doorway. I listened. It was as if she had been swallowed up in the silence of the house. I heard no sound of running footsteps. Nothing.

I sucked in a sharp breath, and the noise of my own action startled me. The room was suddenly alive. A board creaked. There was something, someone, just behind me, just out of sight. My scalp tingled. Ice-cold fingers flicked along my spine.

I spun on my heel. Deidre's door was visible in the light from the landing. It was firmly shut.

The night was going to be long, I told myself. I must keep calm. I made myself look around the room, at the huge lowering shape of the mahogany wardrobe. I went across the room and opened the great doors. Deidre's clothes and the scent of her perfume were so sharply poignant that, for a moment, she was with me.

I shut the doors. Deidre was still trapped behind the doors of her hopeless feeling of inadequacy, of her despair.

And I must continue with my tour of inspection.

I bent and lifted the valance of the bed and peered into the thick shadows beneath. I stood and stared at the vast and shadowy hollow of the four poster bed. There were no sheets turned down tonight, no pink nightdress. The flounced and frilled bedspread was pulled up over the pillows like the sheet over a dead face.

I shivered.

This is no way, I told myself severely, but silently, for I was scared to break the silence, afraid to hear the sound of my own voice. This is no way to carry on! Drink your cocoa.

The note! I had forgotten Alexander's note!

I ran to the dressing table. My reflection ran to meet me, a pale faced girl in black polo-necked jersey and black levis. The face was disembodied. It hung in space, in the silver and black shadows of the room in the mirror. Is that me? Do I really look like that?

I dismissed the stranger who I knew was myself. Alexander had sent me cocoa. Alexander had sent me a note. I was alive. I was me.

I tore open the envelope. I pulled out the sheet of paper. It was the shortest note I had ever received.

I read:

Drink your cocoa. Sleep.

A.

It was the most beautiful letter—that was ever sent to me. He cared. He thought of me. I would do as he said. I was remembered. I was safe.

I put the note back in the envelope and thrust it into the pocket of my levis. I sat down again in the chair that I had pulled to face the door of Deidre's nursery. I held the mug of cocoa in my hands, warming myself more on the note.

I drank the cocoa fast, put down the mug, put my hand on the note in my pocket and settled for the long wait.

My eyelids grew heavy. I jerked them open. I stretched my eyes wide but they wouldn't stay open. As I fell asleep I knew that there had been a drug in the cocoa.

Oh, Alexander . . .

CHAPTER TWELVE

A SINGLE FROND of creeper tapped on the window. On and on, small sharp and persistent, clink-tap-click, a series of toy pellet guns shooting peas against a wooden board.

Danger!

There was cotton-wool where my legs should be. Great bags of black cotton-wool pressed down on my eyelids. Something deep inside the place where my body should be was beating the alarm as if all the bells of hell were ringing.

Hell's bells!

The tapping stopped. The cotton-wool lapped warm and black as the waters of a midnight mediterranean sea. A small breeze whispered.

Whispers!

A man's voice mingled with a woman's voice, low and urgent. On and on, small soft and pleading cry-whisper-sigh, a series of words that pierced my brain with a scurry of electric impulses.

Wake up!

I was there. Somewhere deep in the black waters. I

was fighting the cloying weights. Struggling to rise up. To lift myself. To surface.

My eyes flew open.

I saw her. She was a floating shapeless substance but I knew her. I tried to move. I tried to speak her name. I must have made a drunken sound for her eyes blazed suddenly and she cried in a sharp whisper, 'She's awake!'

A man's shape, his back towards me, head close to hers, dark against gold. No, no, no. Alexander . . .

I was sobbing. I could hear myself but I couldn't stop myself.

'Oh, God!' A whisper, a cry of anguish. 'What am I doing?'

The man's shape, a thicker shadow in the wavering seaweed fronds that floated in the room, covered her, blotted her out. There were blurred sounds.

I blinked.

They were gone. The man and the woman had dissolved in the black waters.

The seaweed fronds were floating in towards me, falling on me. I was being sucked down into my inner being like water swirling down a drain.

Even in my deep sleep I fought until I came up for the second time. For a moment I had forgotten. Shocked, I stared at the strange room. I must still be asleep. I had woken from one dream straight into another. How could I wake myself again? And if I did, might it not turn out that I was in yet another dream? I could go on for ever waking and dying, waking and dying.

Something was different. There was a pallid light where there had been a closed door. The light flowed into the room from a window on the right-hand side. It glinted on the brass rail of an old-time nursery fireguard. In the pool of moonlight on the floor I saw a small figure in jeans. Around the hole at the neck of the emerald green jersey pieces of jagged pink head lay scattered.

I was awake now.

It all came back to me. I was awake but I wished I still slept for the sleeping dream had been easier to bear than the waking nightmare.

I had failed.

It was no comfort to tell myself that I had been drugged. I should not have drunk the cocoa! But, why not? It had come with Alexander's note. *Drink your cocoa. Sleep.* I felt sick. Not with the remnants of the drug that still swam in my bloodstream but with the thought of Alexander's betrayal.

What now?

I could go back, with my tail between my legs, to Aunt Victoria. From there I could do what I had decided to do yesterday morning, pack my suitcase, get in my car and leave Exmoor to the sheep and the ponies.

Leave Alexander?

Without asking him why the hell he had thought it necessary to drug my cocoa? When only last night we had stood facing each other, the spark between us so strong I could scarcely breathe?

Even as I remembered I was out on the landing. I stopped, dismayed. From where I stood the gallery stretched in both directions, longer towards the right, with lights at intervals on all four sides. The red carpeted staircase in the middle of the top passage on my left disappeared into the deep dark shadows of the hall.

There were doors on all four passages of the gallery, all closed. As I looked from one to another they seemed like the teeth of some monstrous animal waiting to swallow me down into the black maw of the hall.

I drew in a deep lungful of air in the effort to clear my mind. There was only one way to find Alexander's room. And I must find it. I must know if my dream had been reality. I must know if Alexander was in his room, or if he had gone with Deidre.

I walked unsteadily on rubber legs on a rubber floor. The walls were billowing curtains blown by a wind that made no sound. The shadows of the well into the hall heaved and sank, but I was moving.

I opened a door that the small working part of my mind told me was beyond Deidre's bathroom. The curtains were undrawn and the moonlight slanted diagonally across the floor. This was clearly the master bedroom. Just as clearly, it was unused. It had the unmistakable feeling of emptiness that goes with the lack of personal paraphernalia. There was a faint musty dampness in the air.

I turned my alien body carefully around and allowed myself a breath of happiness. Alexander didn't sleep in this room. Alexander hadn't occupied this room for a considerable period of time. Alexander had no marital relationship with his wife.

The happiness dissipated.

Alexander wasn't in the room. I had still to find him.

I trod the marshland back past Deidre's bedroom, past the nursery that had no door, onto the passage. Turning to the right I came to a door at the head of the stairs.

I swung towards it. If necessary, I promised myself, I would open every door in the whole of Hawkridge Manor to find its most noble, if disquietingly nonexistent, lord. I was a bit euphoric, enlivened by a breezy blithe spirit that jaunted around somewhere within my drugged mind.

I lurched against the door and opened it with a cry.

'Come out! Come out! Wherever you . . .'

My jaw hung open but no words came out. The room into which my flow of high spirits had propelled me was empty, unlike any room I had ever seen.

It was a large room with whitewashed walls that shone in the brilliant flood of full moonlight. There were no curtains beside the high windows. No carpet on the floor. Against the right hand wall there was a narrow black iron bedstead with a thin mattress, grey rough blankets, no sheets. Against the wall beside the door there was an unpainted wardrobe. In the centre of the bare boards a narrow rug, a praying mat.

But it was the wall on the left that drew me like a magnet. The entire space was bookshelves, rows and rows of books from wall to wall, from floor to ceiling. I looked. Books on yoga occupied the top shelves Then books on Eastern religions, Hinduism, Taoism, the sayings of Mao-Tse-Tung. On the lower shelves books on Judo, karate, kung-fu.

I took out one at random. I opened the flyleaf. In neat small beautifully sculptured letters I read, *Crispin Brett, Hawkridge Manor on Exmoor*. And then a single word that chilled my blood: *Disinherited*.

I began to tremble. The book fell from nerveless fingers. It clattered on the boards and the sound penetrated my mind in an explosion of panic. This was the room of a man governed by a relentless passion, the room of a fanatic who could come back at any moment.

Why wasn't he here now? Asleep on that iron bedstead or sitting in the lotus position on the mat? What was Crispin Brett, Disinherited, doing wandering around on this moonlit night?

Tomorrow is full moon. Deidre's voice repeated the warning but my drugged brain couldn't remember if this was already tomorrow night. *The blue light.* My trembling increased to shudders. What if she had seen it again while I slept and she was, at this moment, being lured—up the valley, up the steep hills, being drawn on by the thing she so greatly feared to the treacherous marshes of The Chains?

I must find Alexander.

The silence of the house zoomed in on me, pressed on my chest until I couldn't breathe. I knew then that I could open all the doors on all four sides of the gallery and look in all the rooms and I would find no one.

I backed slowly. From somewhere I heard little whimpering cries and I guessed that it must be my own sounds but they didn't seem to have anything to do with me.

My outstretched hands behind me found the door. I slid around it, out of that terribly naked room, and my fingers touched a body.

Fear and the drug took over. My heart slammed and I fought like a crazy thing against the soft strong body and the soft steel hold of the arms. I twirled. I dragged away. I tried to run. I reached the top of the stairs. The crimson carpet fell away from where I struggled with the tentacles of steel. Far down below me, at the foot of that endless flight of stairs there was a sea of shadows. I fought the fall into it.

There was pain in my face, sharp and violent.

'Miss Woollacott!'

My brain cleared. I looked into soft and troubled eyes. 'Mary!' Shame coloured my cheeks as deep as the carpet. 'Why didn't you say it was you?'

'I did, Miss.' She grinned. 'You didn't seem to hear me.'

'I'm sorry.'

I stumbled and her arms steadied me.

'Come with me. I'll show you your room.'

I looked at her plain kindly face and nothing made sense.

It must be as I had feared and I had woken from one nightmare into another.

'Come along, Miss Woollacott.'

I yielded. The room to which she led me was the next door along this passage. Mary opened it and I prepared myself for a shock but this room was sweet-aired, the bright chintz curtains were drawn against the night, the sheets were turned back and my familiar, much-worn nightdress lay waiting for me.

'I unpacked for you, Miss.' Mary said.

'Thanks.'

She guided me, firmly, towards the bed. She began to remove my jersey but I stopped her.

'I must stay dressed.'

'Yes, Miss. But you lie down for a while. You look really tired out.'

'I am,' I said.

I let my body fall onto the bed. The pillowcase was lavender scented, cool against my cheek. There were questions to be asked but I couldn't remember what they were. Only one.

'Mary.'

'Yes, Miss?'

'Where is Mr. Alexander?'
'He went out, Miss.'
'When?'
'Soon after he gave me the note and told me to bring you the cocoa.'

Tears scalded the backs of my eyes. I closed my eyelids and was silent, for if I went on asking I knew that I wouldn't like the answers.

'You go to sleep now, Miss Woollacott. There's nothing more you can do. Not until one of them comes back.'

Her voice was already fading.

Something crashed into my sleep, splitting it like an axe in wood. Or a karate chop?

Nerves splitting, I sat up and was out on the floor in a single movement. The door of my room bounced back from where it had been slammed against the wall and I saw that it wasn't Crispin who had come bursting into my room.

Ulysses' huge body filled the doorway. He switched on the light. His hair was a dishevelled ginger mop and there were mud and grass stains up to the knees of his trousers. His eyes were brilliant. He stood a long moment, looking at me. As I felt the full impact of his mind I knew that the waiting time was over.

'Emma!'

My mind was clear and cold. A blackbird was singing a piercing poignant song. Mary, still neat in her dark blue dress and white lace apron, her eyes red with lack of sleep hovered on the landing behind him. I heard the blackbird, I saw Mary, but only on the periphery of awareness.

Ulysses filled the whole of my concentrated attention.

I could feel his thoughts reaching for me, it was an actual physical sensation that held me paralysed. It wasn't fear. It was deeper than fear . . . something that struck at the roots of my individuality. A rabbit will freeze like this, wait, unfighting, for the teeth of the weasel to cut into the jugular vein.

'I'm no rabbit!'

I had spoken aloud, my threatened vulnerable identity striking back at the destroyer. He had been moving towards me but now he checked. He stared at me with lowered head like a hound who has lost the scent.

'What did you say?'

I didn't bother to answer him. 'What time is it?' I asked.

'Time?'

'You know! Tick-tock! At the third stroke it will . . .'

'Emma!'

My moment of supremacy was gone. I controlled the chill that sped over my skin as I saw his eyelids narrow. 'I do want to know,' I said quietly.

He said, without looking at his watch, 'It's nine to six.' Why, I wondered, did he know the time so exactly? And then I forgot everything but the fact that he was coming towards me. 'Thank God you're still here, Emma!'

'Not God.' I said drily. 'Someone . . .' I wouldn't say Alexander. '. . . drugged my cocoa last night.' I hit his eyes with the point of all the frozen terror of the long hours. 'Was it you?'

His eyes gave nothing away. He gripped my wrists and his voice shook. 'Something terrible's happened.'

'To Deidre?'

'I shouldn't've left her.'

'It was you who I saw last night with Deidre.'

'You saw me?' His eyes were narrow slits.

'I saw a man with Deidre. I told you. My cocoa . . .'

He opened his eyes wide and gave me a brief small smile. 'I admit it,' he said.

'The sleeping tablets?'

'That I was with Deidre.'

He was frank and honest, a little pained, so why did I feel that he was playing a game with me, manoeuvring me with Machiavellian skill to some position or place or moment of his own?

'Where is she?'

'She wanted to see it again.'

'Ulysses! Where is she?'

His gaze went right through me. His voice was pitched to a low monotone as if now he was frightened of what he saw within his own mind.

He said, 'I only went out for a breath of air. I kept on asking her to come away but she sat there in a kind of trance. I got cold. I didn't know what to do. I thought if I walked up the hill a short way . . . It was getting light. Walking helps me to think.'

I said, my own voice harsh, too loud in the silence of the house, 'Ulysses! Tell me what's happened.'

'I'm scared, Emma! Scared to hell!'

'It's mutual,' I said icily. 'So just tell me.'

'I saw him, Emma.'

'Him?'

'Alexander.'

I stared up into those blank eyes, defying him. 'Don't be silly, Ulysses!'

'It doesn't make sense! That's what's so shocking.'

'What exactly did you see Alexander do?'

'I didn't see. Not exactly.' His eyes were pleading now. 'To be honest I . . .'

'It'll help,' I said drily.

He went straight on. 'I was afraid to go back. I came over The Chains.' He showed me a trouser leg. 'You can see the evidence of that.'

I looked at the mud and grass stains. 'Yes,' I agreed, 'I can.' But they were there last night. Or had I dreamed it?

Mary, who had been fidgeting in the doorway, controlling herself with increasing difficulty, abruptly came to stand beside us. 'Oh, Miss!' Her voice broke. 'What's going on? Where is Mrs. Alexander? What's happened to her?'

I turned to her. 'Mary . . .'

'I should have watched her last night.' She swung round to Ulysses. 'And I wouldn't've left her. Nor you, Miss. I was waiting on the landing. I meant to stay there. All night. Mr. Crispin sent me to the kitchen.'

'Crispin!'

'Yes, Miss.' She looked back at me. 'He said he'd need some hot soup in a flask and some sandwiches.'

'But why?'

'He often has them, Miss. At night, when he goes to his room.'

I was silent. There had been no hot soup and sandwiches in the bare room. There had been no Crispin. I shook my head a little to myself, for the memory was blurred and I couldn't be certain that it wasn't a dream.

'He sent me away.' Mary's throat was thick with sobs. 'And when I came back she was gone.'

I looked at Ulysses. There was an odd little smile at the corners of his mouth. As if he felt my look he turned from Mary to me and the smile was obliterated in a tight pressure of his lips.

'I think,' I said, 'you'd better take me to Hoar Oak Farm.'

His eyes glittered. 'Did I say that Deidre is there?'

I ignored this. It was of vital importance to keep him guessing about my thoughts, to stay one jump ahead of him in whatever plan he was following. But the answer was so simple. Or was it? It was Crispin who had told me of Ulysses' walks from Hawkridge Manor up past Pinkery Pond and over The Chains to Hoar Oak Farm. It was Crispin who had sent Mary away from her watch in the night, but it was Ulysses who had taken Deidre. Now Crispin had vanished and it was Ulysses who had come back for me.

'I'm right, aren't I?'

'You're a clever girl, Emma!'

He taunted me but he couldn't entirely cover up the flash of alarm. 'Not really,' I said, looking him straight in the eyes. 'Deidre asked me to come here. I took on the whole responsibility of waiting for her. I believed I could help her. I wanted to help her. I failed. If anything's happened to Deidre . . .' I stopped short, my heart slamming against my ribs as I felt again the power of his determination.

'Brave, too, Emma!' he mocked. 'That's some combination!'

'Just obstinate. Pigheaded. Let's go.'

'In my panic,' he said, 'I left my car.' He was walking towards the door. 'We'll have to take Deidre's.'

I turned to Mary and I held her cold hands between mine. 'I'll be in touch with you just as soon as I can, Mary.'

Her face was blotched with tears, her eyes even redder with weeping. 'I've looked after Mrs. Alexander since she came here as a bride.'

Ulysses snarled from the doorway, 'For God's sake, Emma! This is no time for nostalgic tearjerkers.'

I pressed her hands. 'I must go.'

CHAPTER THIRTEEN

ULYSSES DROVE ME in Deidre's Mini. I was uneasily aware of his big body filling his seat, pressing against mine so that I hunched my shoulders and drew away from him. As he slowed for the turn at Simonsbath I felt the sharp stab of another disturbing thought. Whatever lay waiting in Hoar Oak Farm I was wholly dependent on Ulysses. Without my own transport I was trapped.

I said, 'Don't turn.'

He shot a look at me. 'This is . . .'

'I want my own car.'

'That's in Exmoor.'

'Yes.'

'But, Emma . . .'

'I want it, Ulysses.'

'You're mad.'

'No. I just have to be mobile.'

He gave in. He looked at his watch and I momentarily wondered why time was so important and then he was speeding along the empty road. It was the longest five miles I ever went but in five minutes he braked in a skidding stop outside my Aunt Victoria's cottage.

I sprang out. 'It's round the back. I'll be right with you.'

'I'll turn the car,' he said.

My own car started at the first turn of the key. I didn't even look to see if Aunt Victoria was around. It was another life that I had lived with her and I was in a hurry, a great hurry.

I swung out onto the road. The Mini wasn't ahead of me. I stopped and looked over my shoulder. The road behind me was empty. Ulysses had gone.

I slammed my foot down on the accelerator. I'd probably find him around the corner. I didn't. He wasn't anywhere in sight all the way back to Simonsbath. Nor all the way up over the hills.

I swept in and out of swathes of mist, blindingly white in the sun, but I kept my foot hard down for I knew that the danger was not to me, not here on the open road where I was in control of my own steering wheel.

I swept over the cattle grid at Brendon Two Gates with my tyres thundering and the sun in my eyes. Was it still not quite a week since I had walked over the steep grass hills to my first meeting with Alexander?

What lay ahead of me now?

I reached the sharp turn off the road. I changed down and wrenched the wheel. My car held fast and I was bumping and lurching over the long disused track that had been an easy ride for Samphire. Oh, Alexander! I pushed the memory away and concentrated on controlling the steering wheel as it pranced beneath my hands. I looked ahead for Ulysses' car but there was nothing, not even sheep, only the trees and the sweeping empty space of Hoar Oak Hill as it lifted darkly against the sky, concealing beyond its ridge the marshes and bogs of The Chains.

The car charged into the shadow of the belt of trees. I braked and doused the engine. The birds were in full song now but I felt none of their joyous welcome to the day. It was an evil day.

I got out and slammed the door. A blackbird flew screeching into a thicket and, if I could, I would have listened to its warning and run from the derelict and desolate farmhouse in front of me.

But I couldn't.

I looked around. There was no sign of Ulysses' car. I would have to go in through the blank space of the doorless doorway, alone. As if my legs responded to previous commands, I was already walking, quickly, lightly. I reached the doorway. I took a deep breath and walked through it into the room where Alexander had found me sleeping.

What was left of my world fell apart.

The black horses of my father's legend had finally come to Hoar Oak Farm. I recalled my moment of premonition and cried out in a long-drawn silent despair that, although I had felt the warning, I had been unable to do anything to avert the tragedy.

Deidre lay on the floor, where I had slept. I couldn't see all of her for Alexander knelt at her side, his back towards me. But I saw enough. She lay motionless on the cold stone floor. Her body was clothed in a long dress of shrimp pink chiffon. On her tiny feet there were matching sandals. She had fixed a ribbon of the same colour around her forehead and little tendrils of hair escaped from the bandeau. Her head was on the rolled up old grey horse blanket and her hair streamed down beside her shoulders. Her eyes were closed, her lashes lay on her cheeks, thick and dark with mascara. It was as if she had dressed to go to a party.

But the party had ended in death.

I saw him, Ulysses had said.

'Alexander!'

He didn't move. He was so still that I knew he hadn't heard me. I went to him slowly, putting each foot down with care, afraid to break in on him but knowing that I must.

I came to a place beside Deidre's feet. Her hands were together beneath her breasts. Someone had put five primroses between her fingers. Could it be Alexander who had killed her and then laid her out with primroses in her hands?

His head was bowed in his own hands. I could see nothing but the top of his head and the clawing tension in his fingers. My whole being seemed to flow out to him. I put out a hand towards him and caught it back to my side. I didn't care that the evidence I saw could prove him to be a murderer. It wasn't this that held back my hand. I loved him and my love told me that this was his time to be alone. Whether he prayed for his own forgiveness or for Deidre's bewildered soul I couldn't tell. I only knew that I mustn't intrude by the touch of my hand, that contact, physical or mental, must start from him.

As if he felt my thoughts he lifted his head and looked up at me. He stood, slowly, every movement he made was as if his body weighed a ton and his thoughts weighed down on top of his body. He was awash with pain and I was drowning in it.

He looked at me in silence. The silence went on and

on. I could hear it humming in my ears and in my heart. For a long time there was nothing but his eyes watching me, waiting. The moment of nothingness went on and on in a void that only he could fill.

'Deidre's dead.'

'Yes.'

I could hear now, the wind in the trees, the waters in the stream, the blackbirds in the full flighted joy of singing. The void was filled with the turbulence of unsaid things that washed betweeen us, dark and turgid.

Before we could find words to reach across the darkness we heard the crescendoing roar of a car arriving at full speed.

'Ulysses,' I said and felt the blood drain from my heart.

And he answered, as I had done, 'Yes,' for there was no more time for us.

I turned a half step away from him and stared at the doorway.

'Emma.'

'Yes?'

'Look at me.'

The car screeched to a stop outside the doorway. I saw the scarlet bonnet, I saw Ulysses, ginger hair springing up from his head, a flame in the sunrise.

'Look at me, Emma.'

I turned to Alexander and I saw that he was full of a great quietness. He was strong and without fear.

He said, 'I didn't kill my wife.'

'Oh . . . Alexander!'

'It's the truth, Emma.'

'Ulysses,' I gulped, choking with terror, 'said he saw you.'

'Be strong. You must be strong, Emma.'

Ulysses' voice cut between us. 'Yes, indeed, Emma! You must be strong. We must all be strong.'

We turned to him. He exuded excitement. For an instant as the three of us looked at each other we were drawn together, bound by the leaping force of his triumph. And then, so swiftly that I doubted my own understanding, the exultation was gone. He strode across the room, his feet clattering on the bare floor. He stood beside the body of Deidre, his face ashen, staring down at her. He didn't cry out, nor weep. He just stood there, staring, motionless, as if at the sight of her he fell into a coma.

What was going on behind his impassive face? Was he outwardly devoid of feeling, unmoved to the point of callousness because he was what Nanny Dee had said, a changeling with an unhuman set of emotions and reactions? Reason told me that this was a foolish fantasy, but instinct wouldn't listen to reason. There was something inhuman in Ulysses. Either he had a heart of stone, or he had murdered Deidre and knew what he would see when he came into the farmhouse.

I shivered.

Alexander spoke my name quietly, the sound of it ringing in the still room. 'Emma.'

He had come close to me but didn't touch me. The pain was still in him but now it was under control.

'Yes,' I said.

I didn't seem to be able to find anything else to say. In answer to the moment I could only repeat, parrot-like, yes, yes, yes. My failure weighed on me so that I could only look briefly into his eyes and then down at the stone floor.

Alexander said, 'Will you do something for me?'

My eyes flew to his. 'Anything! Anything! You know I will.'

'I know,' he said, his eyes steady on mine. 'Will you . . .'

'Bastard!'

I spun round. Alexander moved a few paces away from me as he said, his voice a whip, 'Be quiet, Ulysses.'

'Quiet! I'll shout it from the rooftops!' Ulysses leaped the intervening space and thrust his face to Alexander's. The blood came rushing into his skin, suffusing the flesh with an ugly red so deep it was almost purple. 'You killed her!'

Alexander held his ground. He kept his face close to his cousin's 'I?' he snapped. 'How? When? Why?'

'You,' Ulysses snarled. 'Because you want Emma.'

I started forward but Alexander's cold face stopped me in my tracks.

Alexander said, 'Go on, Ulysses.'

'This morning. I saw you.' His words began to come faster as if he was launched onto some inner path, impelled by a secret velocity. 'You came here at first light. She was alone. You came in here and you took your stinking horse blanket out of the cupboard and you held it over her face until . . .' He stopped in mid-sentence. The blood drained out of his face and a muscle jerked in the corner of his clenched jaw.

Alexander said, 'Until . . . Ulysses . . .'

The two men held each other's eyes. It seemed to me that Alexander's quiet control was more dangerous than Ulysses' fury. And then, as I watched, my heart trying to beat its way out of my chest, the blood froze in my veins. Beneath the surface fury, Ulysses was as ice-cold as the berg that sent the Titanic to the bottom of the sea. He was charged with the power of absolute self-knowledge.

'Stop it!' I cried. 'Both of you.'

They didn't hear me.

Ulysses laughed. It was an ugly mirthless explosion. 'How the hell should I know how you murdered your wife? That is between you and her.'

'And the postmortem.'

Ulysses turned from him with a swaggering step. 'And my evidence,' he said, 'will put you away. Pity of it is you won't hang.'

I tried again. 'Stop this,' I cried. 'Deidre's dead.'

I didn't exist for either of them. Ulysses stopped beside the empty doorway. He looked out as if he was searching for something but he spoke to Alexander.

'Deidre asked me to bring her here last night,' he said, talking even faster, as if he raced against time. 'It was most helpful of you, Alexander, to dope poor Emma's cocoa.'

I shot a look at Alexander but I wouldn't speak again.

'Go on,' Alexander said, colder than ice. 'Let's have all the facts.'

Ulysses lounged against the doorway. 'Not very many,' he said. 'Circumstantial evidence. You and Deidre have been estranged since the death of your baby, the verdict on which was natural causes. Unless, of course, the coroner links that death with this one. Oh, yes, I know about that one, too. But it's impossible to prove. No motive. Why would you murder your own child when you're so devoutly paternal towards the child you didn't even father?'

I opened my mouth to speak, to shout, to scream, anything to stop the flow of evil that came out of Ulysses, but Alexander glanced at me. His look burned. I bit my lip between my teeth. He turned back instantly to the man lounging against the doorless doorway, and I was silent for the pain was in his eyes again.

Alexander said to Ulysses, 'Have you finished?'

'No.' He turned his head and smiled at his cousin. 'Not yet. I left Deidre here, just as it was getting light. She wanted to spend one last night at Hoar Oak Farm where she was born and reared. Where she lived until fire destroyed her home and left her vulnerable.'

'So . . . you did that, too.'

'I?' Ulysses' laugh rang out again. 'Are you mad?'

'One of us is.'

'Well, it's not me, my dear cousin! I was always the sanest of the three of us. After the fire I watched you in your megalomania. I watched you play the ever-loving all powerful father. The same as you did when we were kids. Nanny Dee and Gammon sent to Kitnore. Mrs. Tamyla—though I sympathised with your disposal of that bitch!—pensioned off in Minehead. Deidre, saved from homelessness, brought to Hawkridge. Only Deidre wasn't the innocent you thought she was. Deidre went happily from bed to bed.'

Alexander hit him. He spun sideways, slamming against the lintel, lurching out of the doorway to fall onto the hard earth.

He lay there, dabbing at the blood that ran from his cut lip. The blood was on his chin, running down his neck, between his fingers. His eyes blazed.

'Temper! Temper!' he chanted and I heard the echoes of childhood in the taunt.

Alexander's fists were clenched. 'Emma,' he said.

And Ulysses went on. 'Another fact for the police,' he said. 'Even in the presence of your dead wife you can't control your urge towards physical violence.' He got to his feet. 'I saw you. It was a long and terrible night. She was mine. She had come away with me. But she wasn't here. She wouldn't move. She sat on the floor. She lay on the floor, staring into space. She wouldn't talk to me. She woudn't let me keep her warm. At last, I could stand no more. I left her. Only for a few minutes, to walk up the hill to get my own circulation going and decide what I must do with her.

'And then I heard your car. I saw you get out and go into the farmhouse. I heard her scream. I heard . . .'

Alexander broke in. 'You saw and heard all this and made no effort to save her.'

For an instant Ulysses hesitated. And then, with a break in his voice, he said, 'I'll never forgive myself. Never! It's no good telling myself that I was up on the hill, too far away when I heard her voice cut off in the middle of a scream. I was a coward. Somehow I shall have to live with myself. My one comfort is that I saw you, Alexander. Because of my evidence you'll pay for the terrible thing you've done.'

He stopped at last.

I dared not look at Alexander. I didn't doubt him, not for a single slamming beat of my heart, but I could think of nothing that I could say to help him. I was paralysed by my own helplessness, sick with the despair of my own poor heart that could only stand by and watch him going down under the flood tide of Ulysses' revenge.

'Emma,' Alexander said again.

'Yes?' In a nightmare I repeated the empty answer.

'Go to Kitnore and phone the police.'

I began to speak but Ulysses' mocking triumph stopped me.

'I've notified the police,' he said. 'In fact, if my ears don't deceive me, they are coming up the track now.'

CHAPTER FOURTEEN

A MAN IS HELPING the police with their enquiries. How many times had I heard this on the radio and TV and never given it more than a passing thought.

Now it dissolved the marrow in my bones.

The police were closely followed by an ambulance. They put Deidre's body on a stretcher and into the loneliness of the ambulance and drove her away in her shrimp pink chiffon party dress with the sad little bouquet of five wilting primroses between her stiff fingers.

The police were official. They put Alexander in the police car. They told Ulysses to follow them to the police station in Minehead where he could make his statement. They asked me a few questions and, when they learned that I had nothing to contribute, they lost interest in me.

The police car drove away along the potholed farm track. I stood, watching it bounce, grow smaller, and I was more lonely than Deidre.

'Poor Emma.'

I started. I had forgotten Ulysses. I turned on him. 'Go to hell!'

He grinned at me. 'Only to the police station. You look cold, Emma.' He opened the door of Deidre's scarlet

Mini. 'Hop in! When I've done my duty as a good citizen I'll buy you breakfast.

I racked my brain for a single withering comment that would destroy him but there was nothing. Ulysses held all the cards. The fact that I knew that he had stacked the pack himself was a useless knowledge without substance to back it. If only I could get under his guard. Maybe if I went to breakfast with him, if I flattered him, I could beat him at his own game and prize a confession out of him.

Maybe he was telling the truth.

'No,' I said. 'I have to go back and tell Mary.'

I braced myself for his argument but he only grinned broader and got behind the steering wheel.

'Good Samaritan, Emma!' he mocked. The scarlet Mini swung around me in a tight circle so that I turned around with it, watching his grinning face. 'Pity you can't bind up the wounds of our beloved cousin, Alexander Brett.'

He set the engine racing. He roared along the track at a rocketing speed that made me flinch for the springs of Deidre's car. But Deidre had no more need to a car. Deidre's body would go from the ambulance to the mortuary to the crematorium.

Where was Deidre? That beautiful fragile lady of the sorrows, where was she now?

I shivered.

Death could be good, even beautiful, as a natural climax to a long life. The death that had come to Deidre was evil and hideous in its violence. As I stood there, alone in the valley beside the derelict farmhouse with the empty hills rising all around me to the sky, I could swear that I felt the touch of a small soft hand. It rested briefly on my shoulder. So vivid was the sensation that I turned my head expecting to see her. I saw nothing. The sensation of physical contact was gone.

And so was my loneliness. Somewhere deep within me, I was comforted, strengthened.

Alexander had said to me, *be strong*. His voice said again, *You must be strong, Emma*.

I'll try, I told him, walking across the deserted space towards my car. I'm not at all sure what to do but I'll be ready to do it when the moment arrives.

The moment didn't arrive.

I wandered through the endless hours of that endless day. I didn't go to Westwater, I couldn't talk to Aunt Victoria. I went back to Hawkridge Manor and talked to Mary. She sat so still, weeping quietly, I could find no words to comfort her. I could only sit and join in her mourning (though I couldn't weep) until, at last, she stopped.

She dried her eyes, blew her nose, stood up and straightened her dress.

'Thank you, Miss,' she said. 'For telling me. If there's anything I can do for you I'll be in Mrs. Alexander's room.' Her smile was watery. 'It'll help to keep busy. I may as well begin putting her things in order. I expect Mrs. Tamyla will be along.'

'Mrs. Tamyla?' I asked.

'Mrs. Alexander's mother.'

'Oh.'

'She doesn't come here much. Mrs. Alexander mostly took Master Jason to visit her mother in Minehead. But I expect she'll come to help me with the sorting out. Well, I'll make a start on it then.'

'Yes, Mary,' I said. 'You make a start.'

We were in the room where I had slept. I had asked Mary to come there as it was the only room in Hawkridge Manor where I felt at ease.

Now I was full of uneasiness. I wandered around the room. There was a green telephone on the table beside the bed. It was a magnet around which I circled, afraid to go out of sight of the instrument. It would ring the moment I was not here and Alexander would reach out for me and I would fail him again.

But at last the tension of waiting wound up into a tight spring and I shot away from the pull of the telephone. I sped down the crimson stairs and across the hall. I tugged at the great door and burst out into the open.

Without thought I kept on running. It was as if my legs tried to keep pace with some inner compulsion. I ran the full length of the house, across the lawn, past the row of empty windows behind which lay the morning room, the ante room and the white drawing room, where Deidre would never have her party now. The emptiness of the rooms seemed to claw at me with invisible fingers as I ran. Where were the servants? Should I have taken it upon myself to gather them together and tell them of the tragedy that had overtaken their mistress? Had Mary told them before she began her ordeal of tidying and sorting?

Where was Crispin?

It was midday. The sun was high in the sky. He had eaten breakfast, Mary had said, but where had he gone since nine o'clock?

I ran off the lawn through a gate in a high wall and into the immense kichen garden. In all of the good earth that was there, no gardener bent to tend his seedlings.

Beyond the enclosed garden I came into the oak forest. I slowed as the trees met over my head. I love trees. They have, for me, a soothing balm. It was instinctively in search of the oak trees that I had come running.

And then I saw it. At my right hand there was a wide track. A hundred yards along the track, leaning drunkenly into a rut left after the tractors and the winter, I saw Ulysses' car.

At the side of the car, staring down at it, stood Crispin.

My foot snapped a twig.

Crispin's white head lifted. He gazed at me for a long moment and then he said, with an elaborate politeness, 'Hallo, Emma, my dear. Very strange.' He shook his head. 'Most odd. I wonder why my boy should leave his car in the wood instead of in the garage.'

'Ulysses is doing a lot of inexplicable things,' I said.

Crispin came close to me, fast. 'What has my son done?' he demanded.

I didn't answer for I was trying to find my own answer. There could be only one reason why Ulysses had hidden his car in the oak wood. He had lied to me. Oh, yes, there had been mud on his trouser legs but it hadn't come from walking over The Chains. Ulysses had *driven* from Hoar Oak to Hawkridge.

'Emma! What has my son done?'

My eyes focussed on him but I answered absentmindedly for I had only one desire. I must talk to Ulysses. Maybe at this moment he was back in the house.

I turned back along the path. 'It's lunchtime,' I said.

He walked at my side. 'Why won't you talk to me, Emma? What *is* going on? I haven't seen Ulysses all morning. Nor Alexander. And Deidre's not in her room. And where have you been, Emma?'

'Where were you last night, Crispin?' I countered.

'Me?'

'You.'

'I was in my room of course.'

I shot a quick glance at him. He looked old. His face was drawn. Remembering the bare asceticism of his room I felt a sharp pity for him.

'Of course,' I said, and added, 'I don't know what Ulysses has done. Only what he says.'

I told him then. He walked at my side with bowed shoulders and uncertain steps. He was a lost creature, a sad nonentity. I dismissed him.

Never have I been more wrong in my judgement of another human being.

Ulysses came back in the late afternoon. I heard the sound of the Mini and ran from my long vigil on the window seat in the white drawing room but I wasn't quick enough. When I reached the front door and pulled it open the drive was empty.

I waited. Wind blew in the trees. Sheep baaed in the pasture to each other. Shadow and sunlight flowed noiselessly down and up the valley and hills. The black line of the dam that held Pinkery Pond seemed to hold up the sky. And I waited.

He came, striding round the corner of the house, his hair aflame in a burst of sunlight. He stopped when he saw me. He looked at me, startled, and I knew that he had forgotten me.

'Where's Alexander?' I asked.

Ulysses recovered. He grimaced as he came to me, leaping up the steps. He said the terrible words. 'Alexander is helping the police with their enquiries.'

I stared at the browsing sheep and the skyful of tumbling white clouds that blew up over The Chains and there was nothing I could say. I felt sick at my own ineptitude but I could only stand and stare while my world and my stomach churned in the boiling pot of the law.

Ulysses said, 'I thought you'd be gone.'

My mind clicked. It wasn't the law I had to break. It was this man standing in front of me, watching me with a curiously intense concentration.

'Well, you were wrong,' I said.

'There's nothing here for you, Emma.'

'Allow me,' I said, elaborately polite, 'to judge that for myself.'

'Alexander won't come back to Hawkridge.'

I kept my eyes on his. 'Did you know, Ulysses,' I spoke lightly, hoping that he couldn't hear the sound of the blood drumming in my head, 'that your car is in the woods?'

His eyes blazed. He took an involuntary step towards me so that his big body blotted out the valley and the hills and his breath was on my cheek.

'Emma,' His voice was low and harsh. 'Go home.'

'I would, Ulysses,' I told him, as sweet as syrup, 'But I have no home to go to.'

'Go, Emma! Go to . . .'

'Hell?'

'If you like!'

'Ulysses,' I said, slow and quiet, 'why do you want me out?'

I saw the flash in the back of his eyes. He moved past me and turned on the step into the house and smiled down on me.

'For your own sake, Emma.'

I mocked him. 'I didn't know you cared!'

'Oh . . . I care.' He was silent and his gaze went over the valley and the hills, over the grazing sheep and the lawn around the house. It came at last back to me. 'I care, Emma. So listen to me. Do as I say. Pack your bag and go away from Hawkridge.'

'Ulysses,' I said slowly, 'are you threatening me?'

It was at this most crucial moment that Crispin came down into the hall. I saw him reach the bottom of the crimson staircase and I was back in the evening I first came to Hawkridge Manor. I saw again, beyond the blaze of light in my eyes, frail in the darkness, the light of Crispin's torch.

He spoke and the time slip was gone. 'Ulysses.'

'Yes, Father.' He kept his eyes on me.

'I have to talk to you.'

'Later,' Ulysses said, looking at me.

'Now, Ulysses.'

Ulysses turned. His voice was like a spear that he threw across the hall. 'Later . . . Father.'

Crispin crumpled. 'Of course,' he said. 'Anytime you're ready. I'll be in my room.'

He turned and began the long tedious journey back up the stairs. Ulysses waited until his father reached the landing and then he said over his shoulder, not turning his head to look at me, his voice a piercing whisper, 'Alexander won't be coming back.'

CHAPTER FIFTEEN

THERE IS A STREAK of obstinacy in me. I had thought of leaving Hawkridge Manor but now I hardened. Wild horses, I told his back as he strode across the hall and took the stairs three at a time, wouldn't drag me from your presence!

The problem was, I discovered, to get back into his presence. At the long table in the dining room that night there were three places laid but only Crispin and I picked at the food and said nothing to each other. When I asked the butler he told us that there had been no message but he understood that Mr. Ulysses was in his room.

I couldn't look at the empty chair where Alexander had sat at the head of the table. In the middle of the meat course I couldn't sit in my own chair. With a muttered apology I pushed it back and left the room and raced up the stairs to the sanctuary of my bedroom.

In a flurry of despair I dragged my suitcase from where Mary had put it against the wall. I flung it on the bed where Mary had already turned back the sheets. I threw my few possessions into it and slammed it shut.

Then I stood and stared at it. I sat slowly, the edge of the bed creaking beneath me. I couldn't make myself pick up the case and walk out of Alexander's house for I would be walking out of his life.

I sat there while the last of the day drained out of the room and the shadows swallowed Pinkery and the high plateau of The Chains. I sat there waiting, not letting myself think, just letting time wash over me, for I knew deep inside that I was waiting for it to begin.

So, although I jumped, I wasn't surprised when something fell against my window pane with the small sharp clatter of a shower of little stones.

My legs were stiff with the long wait and I lurched to the window. The moon had not yet risen but there was a pale luminescence in the sky that showed it was on its way. The clouds had thickened during the evening and now they pressed down on the hills and the valley, filling it with the dark flood of night.

I narrowed my eyelids, straining to see. There was no one beneath my window. I was sure of that, but I was equally sure that somewhere, someone was watching me. I stared into the thick darkness beneath the oak tree and I saw something else. Something that set the blood racing in my veins and my heart pumping in a frenzy of excitement and fear. I felt dizzy. I leaned against the window and made myself draw in five full slow breaths. I closed my eyes. Maybe I had imagined it. I opened my eyes again and it wasn't imagination.

Moving slowly up to the first slope of pastureland where the sheep grazed, flickering, dancing, but going steadily, I saw a will-o'-the-wisp, the blue light that had filled Deidre with terror. She had said that it would be there tonight but Deidre was dead. I froze with fear.

I was fiercely, passionately, eager to stay alive.

And if Alexander was convicted of the murder of his wife?

There was only one answer, only one thing to do. I must follow that will-o'-the-wisp. And if it led me into the marshes up there on The Chains? I shook the thought from me. I was scared enough without letting imagination pierce me with extra jabs.

I cut out on thought. I was running. All of my time seemed to be spent in running. As I skimmed down the stairs my practical self noted that I wore flat shoes, that, because Alexander hadn't come home, I hadn't changed for dinner and was still in black jersey and jeans, so I wouldn't have to hold up trailing skirts or trip over three-inch heels.

The front door was open. I didn't pause to wonder why for the thought had come to me that the small shower of stones was Alexander's way of attracting my attention. I leaped down the white steps and stood impatiently while my eyes grew accustomed to the night and my ears tried to hear beneath the clamour of the wind clattering branches of the oak tree.

'Alexander . . .'

In answer the wind threw a gust of cold air into my face. There was someone. I could feel a presence, an energy, waiting somewhere in the shadows that were taking shape now. I looked up the valley. There was also the blue light, small now, faint and shimmering, already dissipating in the dark of the night. The choice was clear. I could stay around close to the house looking for someone who could prove to be no more than a creature of my own feverish imagination. Or I could follow the light.

I didn't have any choice.

I began to run again. If there was anyone, if Alexander or Ulysses was playing a deadly game of hide-and-seek, he would see me go. My shoulders prickled in anticipation of a hand coming down on me and I ran faster in the vain attempt to outrace my pursuer.

I raced into the flock of sheep, blurred grey shapes that scattered in all directions. One, in its panic, almost hit me and I darted sideways, cursing it for an idiot sheep. It lumbered away with protesting cries and I was thankful to find myself running up the sharp rise to the hedge that bounded the pasture land.

I flung myself over the stile and I was out on the open hillside with nothing but the rising shriek of the wind and the skyful of scudding clouds. I stopped and strained my eyes and ears. I could see nothing beyond the black shadow of the tree that hung over the stile but the sheep were quiet now, there could be no one following me. Unless, of course, it was someone the sheep knew, someone of whom they were not afraid.

I shook myself. To hell with sheep and shadows! To hell with the presence that I knew was somewhere in the night, following me! I would concentrate on catching up with that will-o'-the-wisp that was now beginning to float up the dark slope of the hill.

I stumbled on. I tripped on rough ridges and ruts and sloshed through pools of water but the path was there, leading me on and up, on and up. For a while the wind was quietened by the hill that rose on my left in a huge hippopotamus back against the flying silver-fringed clouds. There was a sharp burst of light. I saw the valley, a couple of feet away from the path on my left, falling away into a deep ravine. I spun on my heel to see the face of the person who stalked me. Even as I turned the clouds closed and the light was gone. My heart missed, paused, thudded. For in that moment I saw a piece of shadow slip forward along the path.

I ran as I had never run before, skidding and stumbling on the rough path. The will-o'-the-wisp ahead of me seemed like a friend. The danger was slipping silently up the hill behind me.

And then, as I clambered, almost on all fours, up the final slope, the blue light rose up in the air, leaped forward and vanished. I stopped and stared. The wind and my blood filled my ears with the pounding of heavy surf. I struggled forward and I was pierced by a flood of ice-tipped arrows of air. The wall of Pinkery Dam was in front of me, a straight line drawn against the streaming clouds. A signpost reared up above me, pointing the way back, the way to the left. No arm pointed ahead for that way led to the marshland of The Chains.

That was the way that I must go.

I walked towards the wall. In the respite of a moment's shelter I knew that the time was almost here. I felt a strange calm as I walked past the gate in the wall and mounted the stile in the full blast of the wind again. As I came down the other side the clouds tore apart. The moon was up. I saw the flat wide green waters of Pinkery Pond in a dip in the land at my left and the flat bright light of the moonshine on the green plateau that stretched before me.

And I saw Crispin Brett. He was only a few feet from me, sitting on the grass, his knees angled sideways, his feet on his thighs. His hands rested palms up on his knees. In the moonlight his hair was a white dandelion seed head and as the wind lifted his hair I thought that it would blow away. He sat motionless. He didn't see me.

At his side, on the grass, there was a small circle of pallid green light. I stared at him. So this was the cause of Deidre's terror, a middle-aged man, a fanatic with a torch who had been going about in the night on his own business and who had never been a threat to her. But I, who had accepted the fear from her mind and made it my own, was in real danger.

I turned away and I froze. There was a man standing on the top step of the stile, a huge towering shape, silhouetted against the sky. He poised motionless, looking down on me from a white mask face in which the eyes were pools of black ink.

The thoughts in my head stopped. For a long long time while my heart executed a single beat I stared into those eyes. I lifted my head a little and I felt the touch of steel ice fingers on my throat. I couldn't move. My feet were rooted in the grass as surely as if I had fallen into the marsh. I knew that time was running out but I stood as motionless as the man, paralysed by the concentrated force of his excitement.

'Hallo, Emma.'

I started. My body, heart and lungs, stomach and knees were leaping machines or lumps of jelly but there was a clear cold bright place in the very centre of my brain.

'It's you,' I said and marvelled at the control in my voice.

The figure leaped down. He came close to me and I smelled the sharp scent of his body. His arms hung loosely at his sides. His shirt was open to the waist, exposing a mass of crisp hair springing from his chest.

The wind took the hair straight back from his head. His face was devoid of expression but I could feel the fire of his purpose as he stood, staring down at me.

'Alexander the Great,' he said and laughed, taunting me.

'Alexander,' I said, not laughing, 'also means protector of men.'

A spasm passed over his face. 'But Ulysses hid in the wooden horse and killed and pillaged and raped the people of Troy.'

The centre of my brain was so cold I felt the bright pain of it. I said, 'How did you do it?'

His eyes cleared and he smiled at me. 'Clever,' he said.

'Tell me.'

'Oh, no, Emma. You're not going to get a last-minute confession.'

I shrugged. 'Suit yourself.' I poured the strength of my will into my jelly-legs and walked a step away and to the side of the huge bulk of man that shut me in. I walked a second step. And a third. 'I'm cold,' I said. If only I could get to the stile before his hand caught me. If only the clouds that had been around on my race up the valley would come back and hide me. 'I'm going back now,' I said and cursed the bright white light of the moon.

'Stop!'

There was an almost childish note of petulance in his voice that set my own hope leaping. 'Why should I?' I asked, walking another step.

'Because I tell you to.'

'Oh, no,' I said, imitating him. 'You're not going to get me with an empty threat.'

'This,' he said, 'is no empty threat.'

My hand was on the stile. I had nearly escaped. But even as the thought went through the clear place in my brain I knew that I had only been allowed to walk to the end of the invisible rope that he was now going to pull tight again.

'Turn around, Emma.'

'And if I don't?'

'But you will. You're a girl with an infinite capacity for curiosity. Or, to put it plainly, you will insist on poking your nose into other people's business. You want to know the answers, Emma. So you'll turn around.'

I turned. He stood where I had left him. He had a revolver in his right hand. It wasn't pointing at me. It lay flat on the open palm that he stretched out towards me, and, as he moved his hand a little, the moonlight caught on the metal and shot a stab of electric light into my eyes.

A part of my fear saw the man still seated on the grass, staring into space and I called his name. 'Crispin! Crispin!'

'He won't hear you, Emma. He won't hear anything that he doesn't want to hear. He's worked at it all his life, and he can cut the outside world in and out at will.'

I looked back and said, 'If I run . . .'

He broke in and for the first time the fire flared in his voice, 'Oh, Emma—you'll run.'

I didn't answer. My throat contracted, my mouth was dry dust.

'That's better,' he said. 'You're beginning to understand.'

I swallowed and licked my stiff cold lips with a salivaless tongue.

'And now,' he said, 'I'll tell you. Deidre was my wooden horse. It was really very funny.' But he didn't laugh. 'It was her idea. A suicide pact, she said. Let's make a suicide pact. The problem was what to do. She didn't want to spoil her image. No blood. She faints at the sight of blood. Besides, she wanted to look beautiful in death, an Ophelia floating down the river of time. She didn't want to be a bore. Every defeated film star takes an overdose and Deidre wanted to be in death what she never was in life, a woman of mystery. So I smothered her.'

A shudder convulsed me.

'That shocks you, Emma? Don't be afraid. My hands won't hold a pillow over your face.'

A question shot up out of my subconscious. '*You . . . did that . . . to the baby . . .*'

His eyes blazed. He looked like a different person as he let rip a violent rage. I saw him as he was and in a moment of terrible knowledge I knew that it can happen, that a human body can be inhabited by a force of violence, by a demon.

I didn't see him move but he was suddenly in front of me. Brilliant with hate and anger his eyes blazed into mine.

'The baby,' he said, 'died a natural death. Infanticide is the work of the devil himself.'

'But murder is acceptable!' I mocked, my voice rasping in my throat.

'When it's necessary, yes, it is.'

'And honour?'

'Honour?'

'You said suicide pact.'

'Don't be naïve, Emma.'

'You never meant to go through with your part of the bargain.'

'I had my own bargain.'

'Your own bargain?' I repeated, playing for time. If I kept him talking I might find an idea appearing in the bright blank space that was my mind, I might think of a way to outmanoeuvre him.

'You're beautiful, too, Emma.'

He smiled at me, a smile that was both cruel and lascivious. It was then that the full implication of his intention came home to me and I began to tremble.

'Two beautiful corpses,' I said, tossing my fear back at him like the shower of pebbles he had thrown at my window to call me out into the night, 'will be one too many.'

His hand came up. My body went rigid. I would not flinch. I would not let him see the depth of my terror.

'Such soft skin,' he said.

He touched my cheek. The tips of his fingers trailed all the way around my face in the caress of a lover. And I took it. I didn't move, didn't flinch. I stared back at him.

I said, charging my voice with contempt, 'You won't get away with two murders.

'Emma Jane Woollacott,' he said, 'following the call of the will-o'-the-wisp. Just as her namesake followed it a hundred years ago.'

My eyes glazed with the concentrated strength of my stare. His windblown hair and moon white face went a little out of focus. 'If you think . . .' I began but I couldn't finish the sentence.

'So you see, Emma. It won't be murder. You followed

the torchlight. In a moment I'm going to throw it out onto the marsh.'

'Do you really think . . .' I challenged. Why was I whispering? Why were we both talking like lovers in the night?

He said, in the silence while I swallowed, 'I *know*, Emma'

'. . . . that I will walk out over the Chains?'

'Run,' he said.

'Run!' I threw the word away. 'No way,' I defied. 'There's no way you can get me to run over the marsh. I'm not a country girl like poor Emma Jane. I don't scare easily.' Then why was I shuddering and quivering? I braced my shoulders and my voice. 'If I did,' I told him, 'I wouldn't be here now.'

'Oh, you've got courage,' he said.

'Thanks.'

'Foolhardy,' he said. 'Only a foolish town girl would be brave enough to come up to Pinkery Pond and The Chains in the dark of the night. Deidre wouldn't.'

My courage plummeted. I was acutely vividly aware of the isolation of this high plateau. The wind had blown most of the clouds away and the full moon sailed free in the sky, a cold silver globe in the navy blue space of the night. The wind blew frigid across the flat grey-green grassland, that looked as safe as the lawn outside Hawkridge Manor, but I knew that both house and plateau were deceptive. I moved on treacherous ground through a world of violence.

He said, 'The three of us were very close. It was fine with us. Until you came.'

'Me?' I croaked.

'You.'

'What did I do?'

'You woke us up out of our long playacting. Phantasy,' he said, 'is a form of creative imagination activity, where the images and trains of imagery are directed and controlled by the whim or pleasure of the moment. We added a third ingredient. Hate. We were tied together, the three of us, plaited in and out of each other's lives like a whip. And we hated each other. *You*,' he accentuated the word, repeated it, '*you* were our catalyst.'

I understood then that he wasn't mad. He knew what he was doing. He had it all worked out. He would drive me until I cracked. He would go on talking in this quiet voice until I screamed at him. He would goad me until my courage ebbed and my mind faltered. Already my nerves were jumping all over my body so that it shook and shuddered and the wind was a thousand needles cutting my face and the noise of the wind was the bellowing and thundering of a stampede of cattle running in my ears.

'Crispin!' I heard my own voice cry out loud and clear.

'He won't hear you.'

'Crispin!' I shouted again.

The squatting figure didn't move. The moonlight poured over his bent white head and into his upturned open palms. My scream echoed on the wind and hammered in my heart, but Crispin Brett didn't hear.

'Emma.'

Against my will I looked back at him. His face was twisted in a savage emnity.

'It's time,' he snarled. Suddenly, with a wide fling of the arm that made me jump away from him, he threw the revolver from him. 'I don't need it anymore,' he said. 'You're ready now, Emma. Let's see if you can find the way through the marsh. Start moving, Emma. Now.'

I began to move, slowly backing away from him, away from the oblivious figure that sat on the grass. I was backing, still, towards the stile. If I could reach it, be up and over it, I would run all the way down the valley, all the way back to Hawkridge.

The huge body moved with the speed of a dragonfly. As it came towards me I shot away from the impact. It passed me, turned and was coming towards me again. In front of it, reaching for me, were two great hands. I stared at them. I could wait for those hands to get me, or I could take my chance on the marsh.

'Run!'

It was an exultant shout, a battle cry, a yell of terrible delight. He stopped a couple of paces away from me. His lips were parted and the moonlight glinted on his teeth. I heard the sickening excitement of indrawn breath and his shout rang in my head.

'Run, damn you! *Run*!'

I spun on my heel and I ran out onto the treacherous grey-green grasses of The Chains, my heart leaping in my throat, my ankles taut as I waited for the step that would sink beneath my foot and send me sprawling into the mud, to lie there choking, suffocating to death.

I heard a cry. I had never heard the cry of a soul in torment and I pray I'll never hear it again. But on certain spring nights when the moon spins fitfully through scudding clouds and the wind is frost-cold on my face I shall for ever hear that cry.

I froze. My mind flipped. I thought it was the voice of my ancestor, my namesake who had run from terror to her death in the marsh, rising up from the dead to warn me.

I caught control of my mind. I turned.

It was Crispin who had cried that terrible cry.

It happened then, fast, in slow motion. Crispin was on his feet. Even as I turned his arm swung in an arc and the torch flew from his hand. The light was still on, it spun in a small spiral of pallid light, a will-o'-the-wisp that was charged with danger.

The huge body of the man waited, as paralysed as myself. For a last instant the wind lifted his hair from around his white face. For an unending fraction of a second the black hollows that were his eyes stared at the will-o'-the-wisp. There wasn't even time for stunned disbelief to change to fear.

The torch hit him full on the forehead. Loud above the wind I heard the crack of bone, the smashing of the skull, the opening of the door for death to enter. He stood there a full second.

And then he fell.

CHAPTER SIXTEEN

I LOOKED AT MY ROOM and there was nothing more to do.

A year had gone by since that night on The Chains but I couldn't go back to Exmoor. My Aunt Victoria had written, almost begging me to visit her for Christmas but I had refused.

There was nothing to go back for.

For times without number I had relived the hours. I did it again now. But I had no hope that I would find hope in the memories.

Crispin took charge. He hurried me, courteously and elegantly careful of me, down the rough paths of the valley, past the scattering sheep, into the house.

He phoned the police. He called Mary to make coffee and sandwiches and, before they came, he poured me a treble brandy that went straight from an empty stomach to my head so that when the Detective Inspector and the Detective Constable and the ambulance men and Alexander came crowding into the white drawing room I was a little inebriated.

It made me cool and aloof and stiff. Alexander looked as aloof as I was. Even allowing for the traumatic effect of the murders of his wife and cousin I was frightened by his withdrawal. We looked at each other like strangers.

Crispin made a statement.

I made a statement.

Everyone except the Detective Sergeant who stayed to watch Crispin went up to The Chains to get down Ulysses' body.

It was then that I went up to the bedroom and Mary came to me with the letter she had found on the nursery mantelpiece.

'Emma,' Deidre wrote, 'I'm writing this while I wait for your sleeping pill to put you out. Ulysses fixed it. Ulysses is coming for me.

'Don't be angry with yourself, Emma, when you wake and find me gone. It's better this way. Ulysses came to me when you were downstairs and we made our decision. You see, Emma, I see it all now. And I don't like myself. All my life, since we were kids I've played the two of them against each other. I wanted security and I wanted love. Some women find the two things in one man. I didn't. So I settled for security with Alexander. I didn't cheat on him after I married him though Ulysses tried! Now I see that, in marrying him without love, I did cheat him. He'll be better without me. So will Jason. I'm going away with Ulysses. A long way away. Neither Ulysses nor I will ever come back to Hawkridge Manor—Deidre.

'P.S. More thinking warns me that I don't entirely trust Ulysses. Our plan is simple. I'm afraid of dying. He will make me unconscious by pressing that vein in the neck and then he'll use a pillow. Then he will swallow the rest of my sleeping pills. A suicide pact is fine if its done together. Ulysses can be following some scheme of his own. I don't know. I'm so very tired. I can't think any more. I just want you to have this letter in case. I can't even think of why. Oh, God Emma, I lied. I was in hell. I had hurt someone. It shouldn't have been Alexander. He was in his own hell when our baby died, without my accusation. Tell him ... Ulysses is knocking. I must open the door or he'll wake you. Forgive me.'

I couldn't think anymore myself. I put the letter in the envelope and into my handbag. I picked up the suitcase I had already packed and walked out of the room. I went down the scarlet carpeted stairs.

I sat in the hall and waited for Alexander.

It was dawn before the police had gone, taking Crispin and Ulysses' body. We talked. Alexander answered all my uncertainties in the aloof voice of a stranger.

He told me that he had gone from Hawkridge Manor early the previous evening. He had left Jason in Minehead with Mrs. Tamyla, but Ulysses' anger and Deidre's collapse had decided him. He drove to Minehead and collected Jason. He had friends in Barnstaple where Jason would be safe from any kidnap attempt. On the way back he fell asleep while driving. He didn't hit anything but he stopped the car and let himself sleep. When he woke he drove to the nearest phone box and phoned Hawkridge. He expected that I would answer the phone but it seemed Ulysses was there, waiting. Ulysses told him that Deidre wanted to talk, that Ulysses and she were going away but that she wouldn't go until she had seen him. That she was waiting for him at Hoar Oak Farm. The rest, he said, you know.

I gave him Deidre's letter then.

He read the letter, folded it, and held it out to me.

I told him to keep it, that it was evidence that supported what I had said about Ulysses' confession in my statement.

And after that there was nothing more to say. A mist had come down from the moors and drowned Hawkridge Manor. When Alexander opened the door a ghost came swirling in and other shadows and shapes shifted in a blank white crowd around the porch.

My car was a small dark lump.

'I have to go,' I said.

This time it was Alexander who said, 'Yes.'

It was all he said.

I saw him at the inquest. He was cool, aloof and stiff. He thanked me for my evidence and when I asked after Jason he said, 'The boy's all right' and turned away with his solicitor.

There was no trial. Crispin Brett died. He didn't go on a hunger strike, he didn't kill himself, he just stopped living. Not suddenly or dramatically. It took him seven weeks. The police doctors called in Dr. Hallet but not all the Queen's men could put Crispin Brett together again. His will had turned from life to death. He used all that he had learned and he died.

Alexander sent me a formal letter to tell me of his Uncle's death and to advise me that I wouldn't be needed for any trial. And that was the end.

I absorbed myself in my work. I made myself take part in the life of the University outside my work. I joined in all the hours of talk and the drinking of beer.

I accepted an invitation to stay with a girlfriend for Christmas and we went for a week's skiing in Austria. After that I was broke and there was only my work.

And my foolish aching heart that couldn't, wouldn't listen to the hours of old-fashioned common sense with which I tried to control my longing. If only I knew that Alexander was well and happy and living.

I couldn't ask Aunt Victoria. When she wrote, Aunt Victoria studiously avoided any hint of reference to Alexander Brett.

So here I was, on the eve of The Day of The Hobby Horse, alone and miserable, sitting around and thinking, waiting for the impossible.

The impossible happened.

The phone rang and it was Alexander.

'Emma.'

His voice was warm and personal and relaxed. 'Alexander,' I said, tears falling about inside me. 'Where are you?'

'Just round the corner. We can pick you up in a couple of minutes. I thought I'd better ring first. In case you don't want to see us.'

'Us?' The tears fell down my cheeks.

'Jason and me.'

'I want to see you. Both of you.'

'He'd like to talk to you.'

'Put him on.'

There were sounds of rustling and low chatter and then Jason's high young voice. 'Hi, Emma.'

'Hi, Jason.'

'Are you going to come with Daddy and me?'

'Yes.'

'Super! Then we can all go see the Hobby Horse together.'

'Yes, Jason, we can.' The tears blurred my eyes.

'Daddy's given me my own drum. I've got it in the car. I'll play it for you.'

'All the way to Hawkridge Manor!' I laughed in between my tears.

'Daddy wants to talk to you.'

More rustling, and then Alexander said, 'Don't be frightened, Emma. I won't let him beat the drum more than half the way to Hawkridge Manor.'

'Oh, Alexander, I don't know what to say.'

'Don't say anything. We've got all the time in the world. See you in two minutes.'

I heard the phone go down. For a long moment I could only stand there. And then I realized what he had said. I slammed down the phone. I raced around, shutting windows, looking at gas taps wiping my eyes, pushing a clean handkerchief and my toothbrush wrapped in tissue in my handbag.

The horn tooted.

I didn't even look around. I ran from my lonely life without a backward glance.

They were waiting for me on the pavement, side by side in the morning sun. Jason had his drum around his neck and, as I appeared, he beat out a tattoo that I thought was remarkably talented.

His father put a hand on the boy's shoulder and Jason stopped.

His father?

I looked up at Alexander. We would never know now. Alexander came to me and took my hand in both of his. He didn't kiss me but it wasn't important.

Jason cried, 'Come on, you two!'

He turned and strode back to the Jenson. The answer was in front of my eyes. The proud lift of the child's head, the assurance in the dark eyes, the charm and arrogance of his command all proved his inheritance. This child could only belong to Alexander.

Alexander said, 'Are you ready, Emma.'

'I'm ready, Alexander.'

As we got into the car I seemed to hear Deidre's voice, *I didn't cheat Alexander.* And I answered her, *Rest, Deidre, I won't cheat him either. I love him.*

The car moved away from the kerb.

Jason said, 'Can I beat my drum now, Daddy?'

'When we get out of the town.'

'Okay! Step on it! I want to get home.'

'Patience,' Alexander said. 'We'll get there.'

There are a lot more where this one came from!

ORDER your FREE catalog of ACE paperbacks here. We have hundreds of inexpensive books where this one came from priced from 75¢ to $2.50. Now you can read all the books you have always wanted to at tremendous savings. Order your *free* catalog of ACE paperbacks now.

ACE BOOKS • P.O. Box 690, Rockville Centre, N.Y. 11571

D.E. STEVENSON ROMANCES

"Finding a re-issued novel by D. E. Stevenson is like coming upon a Tiffany lamp in Woolworth's. It is not 'nostalgia'; it is the real thing."

—THE NEW YORK TIMES BOOK REVIEW

ENTER THE WORLD OF D. E. STEVENSON IN THESE DELIGHTFUL ROMANTIC NOVELS:

AMBERWELL
THE BAKER'S DAUGHTER
BEL LAMINGTON
THE BLUE SAPPHIRE
CELIA'S HOUSE
THE ENCHANTED ISLE
FLETCHERS END
GERALD AND ELIZABETH
GREEN MONEY
THE HOUSE ON THE CLIFF
KATE HARDY
LISTENING VALLEY
THE MUSGRAVES
SPRING MAGIC
SUMMERHILLS
THE TALL STRANGER

ROMANTIC SUSPENSE

Discover ACE's exciting new line of exotic romantic suspense novels by award-winning author Anne Worboys:

THE LION OF DELOS

RENDEZVOUS WITH FEAR

THE WAY OF THE TAMARISK

THE BARRANCOURT DESTINY

Coming soon:

HIGH HOSTAGE